Praise for the novels of bestselling, award-winning author Catherine Kean

Dance of Desire
"On a scale of 1-5 stars, this is definitely a 6 star book! . . . Don't miss this one!"—6 stars, *Affaire de Coeur* Magazine

My Lady's Treasure
"Filled with lively characters, a strong, suspenseful plot and a myriad of romantic scenes *My Lady's Treasure* is a powerful, poignant tale that will keep readers turning pages until the very end."—5 stars and Reviewer's Choice Award, The Road to Romance

A Knight's Vengeance
"Kean (*Dance of Desire*) delivers rich local color and sparkling romantic tension in this fast-paced medieval revenge plot."—*Publishers Weekly*

A Knight's Reward
"Ms. Kean has done it again with her talent to capture the reader's attention with all the elements of a must-read. The opening pages are filled with a wonderful tension that sets the stage for a great story."—Fresh Fiction

A Knight's Temptation
"…an entertaining medieval romance brimming with sass, action, adventure, and lots of sexual chemistry."—*Booklist*

A Knight's Persuasion
"…stirring adventure, superb characters, and enticing heroes. Ms. Kean continues to snag the reader with her fast-paced tales of heroic knights."—4-1/2 stars. *Affaire de Coeur* Magazine

Books by Catherine Kean

A Knight and His Rose
A Knight to Remember (Novella)
A Legendary Love (Novella)
Bound by His Kiss (Novella)
Dance of Desire
Her Gallant Knight (Novella)
My Lady's Treasure
One Knight in the Forest (Novella)
One Knight Under the Mistletoe (Novella)
One Knight's Kiss (Novella)
That Knight by the Sea (Novella)

Lost Riches Series
A Knight's Desire (Book 1)
An Outlaw's Desire (Book 2)

Knight's Series Novels
A Knight's Vengeance (Book 1)
A Knight's Reward (Book 2)
A Knight's Temptation (Book 3)
A Knight's Persuasion (Book 4)
A Knight's Seduction (Book 5)
A Knight's Redemption (Book 6)

Boxed Sets
The Knight's Series: Books 1-5

Paranormal Romances
A Witch in Time
Hot Magic

One Knight's Kiss

A Medieval Romance Novella

By

Catherine Kean

One Knight's Kiss © 2016 Catherine Kean

Cover design by Dar Albert, Wicked Smart Designs

Cover photo copyright © Period Images

ISBN-13: 978-1544162225
ISBN-10: 1544162227

Also available in eBook.
ASIN: B01NBSEBGA

Catherine Kean
P.O. Box 917624
Longwood, FL 32791-7624
www.catherinekean.com

Dedication

For my parents, David and Shirley Lord, who taught me the joy and magic to be found within the pages of books.

Chapter One

The town of Wylebury, Hertfordshire, England
December 22, 1209

"I s that a book?" Standing at a merchant's table laden with fragranced soaps, Lady Honoria Whitford leaned sideways to better see what appeared to be a leather-bound tome lying on a blanket spread on the ground just a few paces away. Market shoppers moved past with their baskets full of goods and blocked her view of the peddler and his wares.

Honoria set down the soap she held. Her pulse fluttered with excitement, for her collection of books was her greatest treasure. She'd frequented the shops at Wylebury since she was a girl, and 'twas rare to find a tome for sale. She must be quick, or someone else would buy it before she could.

Pushing back the hood of her woolen cloak, she tried to locate her older brother, Radley. He'd escorted her and a ward of their late father's who lived at Ellingstow Keep, sixteen-year-old Lady Cornelia de Bretagne, to the town for the last market day before Christmas. They'd wanted to purchase gifts, to be given on Christmas Day, as had become the custom at the castle. Merchants had all kinds of lovely items for sale, including exotic spices to flavor holiday dishes, painted figurines, table linens, and beribboned bunches of

1

mistletoe. The scent of freshly-baked mince pies wafted from the baker's shop.

Radley had arranged to meet up with a nobleman named Tristan de Champagne, whom he'd befriended years ago when they were both squires at the same castle in Lincolnshire. They'd trained together to achieve knighthood. While Honoria had never met Tristan before, he'd be spending the holidays with them at Ellingstow.

Rising up on tiptoes, Honoria searched the throng for her brother. Some parts of the market square were obscured by smoke from fires where folk had gathered to warm themselves on the clear, wintry day. Radley had told her and Cornelia that for their safety, they should stay together at all times. One of the armed guards who had accompanied them on the day's journey was near Cornelia, though; she was stacking soaps into a pile and wouldn't want to leave her shopping to go with Honoria to see the peddler's offerings.

If Honoria was quick, she could buy the book and be back before Cornelia even noticed she'd gone.

Honoria motioned for another Ellingstow guard, who was holding purchases handed to him earlier, to follow her, and went to the peddler sitting on the ground with his hodgepodge of wares. The man, his hair unkempt, his garments torn and stained, scrambled to his feet and bowed to her.

Her sire would have handed this poor soul a few coins to at least get some fare, especially at this time of year, when 'twas important to think of those who were less fortunate.

Oh, Father. How very much I miss you.

Forcing aside her anguish, Honoria reached past the earthenware candle holders, bent hairpins, and assorted wooden toys and picked up the book.

The plain, brown leather cover wasn't at all

remarkable. When she opened the tome, though, the piquant scent of parchment wafted to her: a smell that signified fascinating discoveries, grand adventures, and limitless knowledge. Joy tingled through her as she carefully turned the pages and glanced over the drawings and notes. The book contained the personal writings of a noblewoman who had managed a keep while her lord husband was away on Crusade with King Richard the Lionheart.

Feeling the weight of the peddler's stare, Honoria asked, "How much for this book?"

"'Tis not fer ye, milady."

"'Tis for sale, is it not?"

"Aye, but—"

"I have money. More than enough, I vow."

The peddler's grubby fingers twitched, as though he was counting out coins. Then he scowled and held his hand out for the book. "As I said, 'tis not fer ye."

Honoria simply *had* to have it; 'twould be the perfect addition to the small collection her sire had given her before he'd died. Also, she was eager to know more about the lady who had taken such care to document her life's accomplishments. One day, Honoria hoped to marry, and then she would be responsible for running her husband's fortress when he was away visiting other lords, inspecting his estate, or attending meetings in the great city of London; she could learn a great deal from another lady's experiences. "Please," she insisted. "Kindly tell me the price."

"Fine. Thirty pieces o' silver."

"*Thirty* pieces?"

"Robbery," a man said from behind her. "Unless that book is penned in gold."

Startled, she glanced over her shoulder. A broad-shouldered man with dark-brown hair that brushed his shoulders stood a few paces away. He was very handsome; as beautiful, she was sure, as the heroic knights in the book of romantic tales she'd inherited from her sire. The stranger was obviously a nobleman, for his black cloak was of fine quality. A sheathed sword rested at his left hip. As his steady, brown-eyed gaze held hers, a shiver trailed through her. Fighting an odd feeling of breathlessness, she focused again on the peddler.

"The book is special." He held out his dirty hand again.

"What is so special about it?" The nobleman's voice was deeper than Radley's, and had a slight rasp that made Honoria think of a dagger grazing a whetstone. Yet, 'twas the deliberateness of his words that made her uneasy.

Had he recognized what a prize the book was? Did he want to buy it, too? Well, she wouldn't let him; she'd seen it first.

Still holding the tome, she glanced about for her brother again, in case she needed his help. Relief washed through her when she saw him talking with her guard. She would have heard Radley's voice earlier, but his conversation was being drowned out by men haggling with a wine seller.

"The book, milady," the peddler insisted. "I will not change me price."

The nobleman moved closer. "May I see it?"

Part of her immediately protested. Yet, the tome didn't belong to her. Not yet, anyway.

She handed it to him. He opened it, the binding creaking slightly, and flipped through the pages. As he angled the book to better see a drawing, she saw that the cover had been damaged at some point and repaired; the leather buckled slightly along the back edge.

That didn't matter to her, though. The damage was part of the provenance of the tome.

The nobleman shut the book. "While I am no expert on tomes, I see no reason for the extortionate price."

Sweat beaded on the peddler's brow. "I 'ave a livin' ta

make."

"As do all merchants in this market. Overpricing of goods, however, is a crime. Shall I find the sheriff and tell him the price you asked of the lady? This tome cannot be worth more than a few pieces of silver."

The peddler's gaze darted away. Honoria followed the direction of his glance to see another man had stopped to watch what was going on. A puckered scar slashed down the onlooker's face. Catching Honoria's gaze, the man nodded in greeting and then stooped to pick up a candleholder.

"Please," the peddler whined, "I do not want trouble."

Honoria reached for the coin purse she wore on a long cord around her neck. "I will give you five pieces of silver for the book,"—she tipped money into her palm— "and five more, so you can buy food and clothes."

"'Tis a generous offer," the nobleman said firmly. "I suggest you take it."

The peddler hesitated, what looked like fear in his eyes, but then snatched the money.

Smiling, Honoria tucked the tome under her arm. The book was hers.

The lady was clearly thrilled with her purchase. Happiness sparkled in her hazelnut-brown eyes.

A raw ache gripped Tristan, for Honoria's winsome smile reminded him of his former intended's. Lady Odelia Putnam had captivated him with her beauty, won his devotion, and then, three months ago, had crushed him as if their relationship had been a frivolous game—not the beginning of a lifetime together. While he hadn't loved her with the all-consuming passion some couples experienced, he *had* cared for her, enough to ask her to be his wife, and her shocking betrayal had been akin to being stabbed through the heart.

Thankfully, his heart had been hardened by other experiences in his twenty years of life. Odelia had wounded him, but not destroyed him—and he'd vowed never to be that vulnerable ever again.

Aware Honoria was still smiling at him, he managed a smile back.

"Thank you, milord," she said.

Tristan bowed; he might be bitter, but he'd always be chivalrous when in the presence of a noblewoman. "My pleasure, Lady Whitford."

"How do you know my name?" Her eyes narrowed. "Are you Tristan?"

"I am indeed. Your brother pointed you out to me. When I heard your conversation, I felt obliged to step in."

Setting his hand at her waist—a bold move, when they'd only just met, as her astonished expression conveyed—Tristan guided her away from the blanket. Working for the past four years as a bodyguard for a wealthy merchant in the town of Lincoln had taught him to rely on his instincts; they'd never failed him, and were warning him now to put distance between her and the peddler, as well as the man with the scar who was lingering nearby.

Tristan escorted her to the soap table, where Radley joined them. "I see you have met Tristan, Sis."

"He was a lot of help moments ago." Honoria gestured to the tome.

"*Another* book?" Radley groaned. "You already have four."

"I plan to have many more," she said with a cheeky grin. "A whole shelf of them."

She was exquisite when she smiled. Dimples formed in her cheeks, and her creamy skin glowed...and Tristan damned well hated the interest stirring inside him. Once Christmas was over and he'd moved to London to become the personal guard of one of England's leading goldsmiths, who was also close friends with King John, Tristan's duties would keep him far too busy to fall in love again.

A pretty, blond-haired woman wearing a fur-trimmed cloak and holding a cloth bag turned away from the soap table. A faint scar blemished her cheekbone—an unusual injury for a young lady. "A whole shelf?" she asked. "Of what?"

"Books," Radley told her. "What else would Honoria want?"

The younger woman rolled her eyes. "I should have guessed."

"Oh, cease your teasing, you two," Honoria said with a chuckle.

The younger lady noticed Tristan. Her blue eyes lit with interest, and her gaze wandered rather brazenly down the front of his cloak. "Forgive me for being bold, but are you Tristan?"

"I am." Before he could bow, she thrust out her hand. He couldn't ignore it, not unless he wanted to risk causing offense.

Taking her slender fingers and raising them to his lips for a quick kiss, he asked, "And you are?"

"Cornelia de Bretagne."

Tristan tried to pull his hand free, but she curled her fingers around his. She held on far longer than was necessary or appropriate, before, with a coy grin, she finally released him.

"Well," Tristan said, "I am delighted to have finally met the ladies Radley has told me so much about."

"What did he say?" Cornelia mock-frowned. "You must tell us."

"After a few goblets of wine, I might," Tristan

agreed, eliciting an indignant cry from Radley. "Truth be told, I am very much looking forward to spending Christmas at Ellingstow."

"We are thrilled you will be joining us." Cornelia fluttered her lashes.

Honoria frowned, as if she were growing weary of the banter. "Are we finished shopping at the market? If so, I suggest we start our journey home."

"A wise idea," Radley agreed. "I do not like to think of Mother fretting. Yet, after what happened to Father, she will be worrying about us until we ride back through the castle gates."

Tristan had heard of the brutal attack on Lord Lewis Whitford, and how Radley had inherited his sire's estates at a far younger age than he'd ever expected. Radley was intelligent and capable, though, and Tristan had no doubt he was managing his duties well.

Movement drew Tristan's attention to the stall next to the soap table. The man with the scarred face was browsing the goods. He was close enough to hear what they were saying, if he wanted to eavesdrop.

Misgiving trailed through Tristan. *Was* the man listening in on their conversation? If so, why, and what did he hope to learn?

The man strolled on to the next merchant's table, and Tristan shrugged off his sense of disquiet. He was probably overreacting—a consequence of his profession. Still, 'twould be safest if they left the market.

"Heading for Ellingstow sounds like a grand idea," he said. "Radley, where did you tether your horses? I will fetch my destrier and meet up with you there."

Chapter Two

Browned leaves skittered down the dirt road through the forest as Honoria and Cornelia rode their mares side by side. Two guards on horseback were a short distance in front of them, and two rode behind, where Radley and Tristan were conversing.

Whatever they were discussing was impossible to hear over the clatter of the horses' hooves—convenient for the men, but Honoria would love to know what they were talking about. Matters of estate, mayhap?

Radley had had tremendous responsibility thrust upon him when he'd become lord of Ellingstow five months ago, upon their sire's death. Their father had been gravely wounded while escorting a crown official to a gathering of lords who'd wished to discuss King John's constantly-increasing taxes, as well as the sovereign's seizure of a local estate and expulsion of the respected family who'd lived there.

Her sire, who had been granted Ellingstow by the King years ago, had hoped that the meeting would resolve some of the discontent among his peers; he'd believed the worst outcome for England would be a bloody uprising. The convoy had been attacked less than a league from the meeting site, and Honoria's father, the only survivor apart from his wolfhound, had soon perished from his wounds. The assailants had not been captured, despite the local sheriff's investigation.

Honoria's mother, Valerie, had been devastated by her husband's death, but had committed to helping her son succeed as the new lord. She'd called upon close family friend and widower Guillaume de Bretagne—Cornelia's father—to help Radley forge necessary alliances. 'Twas not long before Guillaume began courting Valerie; soon, they'd likely be betrothed.

Sadness pressed upon Honoria, for so much had changed since her sire's death. There had been other ambushes in past months; more wives left without husbands, more children without fathers. A chill ran through her, and she glanced out into the woods, where some of the shadows were as black as midnight. While the guards from Ellingstow were well-trained, and Radley and Tristan were also skilled fighters, she couldn't wait to be safely within the keep's walls.

An irritated sigh drew her gaze to Cornelia. Seated side-saddle upon her horse, the younger woman shook out more of her skirt. "My gown will be badly creased when we reach the castle."

Trust Cornelia to be worrying over something as inconsequential as her gown. "You will still look lovely," Honoria said.

"I might change my bliaut. I do want to look my best for our guest."

A tiny tingle of jealousy flared within Honoria, but she brushed it aside. She wasn't the kind of woman who would interest a man like Tristan. She was nineteen, thus older than most unwed ladies. She was also too plain-looking, too quiet, too…unremarkable—unlike Cornelia, whose waist-length hair wasn't ordinary brown but lustrous gold. The young woman was an exquisite beauty.

"Tristan *is* most comely, is he not?"

"He is." Honoria adjusted her grip on her horse's reins. "You were rather forward, though, in the market."

"I was being friendly."

"You had only just met him—"

"—but I intend to get to know him very well over Christmas."

The last time Cornelia had pursued a lord, she'd ended up in tears for days. Honoria, hating to see her friend so miserable, had done her best to comfort the younger woman, even offered to read her some of the old tales from her book, but Cornelia had preferred to sulk.

Honoria must have made some small sound of dismay, for the younger woman giggled. "Do not be so concerned."

"I am worried about you."

"Worried?" Cornelia snorted. "I am ten-and-six. Many ladies my age—and yours—are already married and bearing babes. They are overseeing castles for their rich husbands and being invited to feasts and other marvelous celebrations. I want that for myself."

What lady *didn't* want to be in that position? 'Twas the perfect life, if she and her husband were deeply in love. The holiday season would be especially wonderful. Honoria glanced out into the forest again, her eyes burning. Her sire had told her more than once that he looked forward to the day he'd grant her hand in marriage to a lord who'd cherish her. Her father had died with her unwed and without a suitor.

"Why have you gone quiet? Do you disapprove of what I want for my life?"

"Of course not." Honoria managed a smile. "I hope you will find true love and be very happy."

The younger woman's expression turned sly. "What if I find those things with Tristan?"

Honoria suppressed another unwelcome stirring of jealousy. She didn't have any claim to Tristan; he might already be betrothed and soon to wed. "I do not know if he is seeking a wife or not. Yet, if he ends up being the right man for you, then your love was obviously destined to be."

"Like the romances in your musty old book?"

The tome wasn't musty, but Honoria chose not to correct Cornelia. "Exactly like those stories."

The younger woman smoothed her hair. "Well, I cannot *wait* to see what happens in the next few days."

"I did not realize the situation with your father was so dire," Radley said.

Tristan's leather glove creaked as he clenched his hand, resting on his thigh, into a fist. "I have not spoken to my sire in many weeks. The last time I saw him, he told me he was gravely disappointed in my actions, and that I was a disgrace to the de Champagne family."

Radley whistled softly. "Even though you were not the one at fault?"

"Aye." Memories of the night he'd walked in on Odelia and her lover, half-naked and locked in a passionate embrace, were burned in Tristan's mind. He'd never forget the moment she'd torn her mouth from the young lord's. She'd been so calm and self-righteous when she'd straightened her gown, as if she'd had every right to do what she pleased—despite knowing that Tristan had planned to ask her father for her hand in marriage the following morning.

It had taken tremendous effort for Tristan to walk away, rather than pummel the other man until he'd collapsed unconscious on the floorboards. Tristan hadn't told her sire of the incident; a knight never besmirched a lady's reputation. Tristan hadn't intended to tell his own father the truth, except that his sire had goaded it out of him.

"My father insisted I should have married Odelia anyway," Tristan said with a harsh laugh. "If she was with child, I should have claimed the babe as my own, especially if 'twas a son."

"God's blood. Why?"

"I would have had a legal heir, and thereby would have secured the de Champagne estates."

"'Twas the only reason? To secure your family's legacy?"

"Not quite. Since Odelia's sire and four brothers are well-known in London, my father…said their influence would have been of great benefit to our family."

"Ah." Radley spoke the word as if it tasted vile.

"I have no doubt my sire expected, once she and I were wed, that I would help secure favorable positions for my own brothers."

Radley shook his head. "Your father expected too much."

"He does not believe so."

"You were naught but chivalrous in your relationship with Odelia, and she betrayed you."

She had indeed. But, she'd also taught him a valuable lesson. He had no control over someone else's decisions, but he could damn well govern his own. His duty had never failed him—and being married to his career was far safer than risking betrayal again. His sire expected his sons to excel in their careers; one day, he would understand and accept Tristan's reasons for rejecting Odelia.

"What do your brothers think about this situation?"

Tristan's father was a formidable, domineering man who could bring seasoned warriors to tears; he knew how to keep his sons under his control. "My siblings, at least for now, are not choosing sides. I do not believe they agree with my sire, but they are also reluctant to challenge him."

"Well, I say 'tis bloody rotten of them not to rally behind you."

Warmth spread through Tristan's chest. He'd always be grateful for Radley's loyalty and friendship. "You see now why I did not want to spend the holidays at my sire's castle."

Radley grinned. "'Tis his loss. We will have a fine celebration at Ellingstow. 'Twill be the rowdiest, most memorable Christmas ever."

Tristan chuckled and looked ahead at the two ladies. Honoria's braided brown hair fell in a glossy rope down the back of her cloak, and her face was turned to him in profile as she spoke to Cornelia. God's bones, but Honoria was lovely. Her features weren't as perfect as Cornelia's, but she had her own unique beauty, and she intrigued him.

Yearning again wove through him before he hardened his heart against the foolish emotion. Of one thing he was certain: This Christmas would *not* see him caught up in a new romance.

Honoria's gray-haired mother was walking across the bailey, her blue cloak drifting in the late afternoon breeze, as they rode out of the shadows of the gatehouse. Her ladyship smiled and waved. Honoria waved back, pleased to see that Willow, her late sire's wolfhound that had become Honoria's beloved pet, was at her mother's side. Honoria had told the dog earlier to stay close to her parent.

"I am so glad you are home," Lady Whitford said, as Honoria and Cornelia halted their mares. The others reined in their horses, and stable hands set down wooden blocks to help them dismount.

Honoria held her book flat against her bosom; she

didn't want to accidentally drop it. She slid down from her horse to join Cornelia.

"Mother." Radley kissed Lady Whitford's cheek. "May I present my dear friend, Tristan de Champagne."

"'Tis a pleasure." Her ladyship dropped into a curtsy.

Tristan bowed. "I am honored to meet you. Thank you for letting me impose upon you at Christmas."

Lady Whitford laughed. "You are not imposing."

"Of course he is not," Cornelia cooed. When Tristan glanced at her, she beamed.

Radley scratched Willow's ear that had been slashed when she'd defended their sire during the attack. "All went well today, Mother?"

"Aye. I just came from discussing the Christmas Day feast with the cook."

"Ah. And?"

"He is preparing seven separate courses, and will cook frumenty and other dishes that will go with the boar you will be hunting on the morrow. He is also creating a subtlety for the final course. He is calling it the Winter Swan. 'Tis the most impressive sculpture of pastry and marzipan I have seen in a while."

"You clearly have matters well in hand," Radley said.

"Well, I am happy to organize the feast, since I did so when your sire was lord. Sydney has also been busy overseeing the collection of rents." She gestured to the steward, near the kitchens with the captain of the guard and several men-at-arms; they were helping folk who'd brought loaves of bread, chickens in twig cages, and earthenware jugs of ale—fare owed to Radley by all of his tenants at Christmas. The food would in turn be used to make a meal at the fortress for the peasants on Christmas Day.

A chill wind gusted through the bailey, and Honoria worried for her mother, who drank infusions every day to ease her aching joints and had been told by the castle's healer to stay indoors as much as possible. "Why do we not go sit by the hearth? We can warm up while we talk."

"What a good idea," Lady Whitford agreed.

"I will show Tristan to his chamber, so he can unpack," Radley said. "Then we will meet you in the great hall."

"All right." Honoria slid her arm into her mother's, because sometimes her parent needed help climbing the forebuilding stairs.

Honoria's skin suddenly prickled with goose bumps; she *knew* Tristan was watching her. When she glanced at him, his mouth ticked up at the corner—not an arrogant smile, but one tinged with admiration.

She'd thought he couldn't possibly be any more handsome, but right now....

Heat pooled in her belly, the sensation unfamiliar but thrilling. She longed to speak, to break the charged silence, but didn't know quite what to say.

Whining, Willow pushed her nose against Honoria's free hand.

As though the dog had broken some kind of spell, Tristan turned and strode to his destrier, with Radley and Cornelia following close behind.

Tristan patted his horse's lathered neck then set to work untying his saddlebag. Honoria's loveliness lingered in his mind. Even more compelling, she was a compassionate soul who cared very much for her mother—yet another thing he admired about her.

'Twas a dilemma how much Honoria intrigued him. He *didn't* want a relationship, so why did he feel so strongly about her? What mysterious hold did she have over him?

Stealing a glance at the keep, he saw her and her mother enter the forebuilding and the iron-banded door shut behind them. His own mother had perished from sickness when he was six years old. He could no longer recall her features, but remembered how her smile had comforted him, and how her hugs and kisses had been bestowed with much love.

Eighteen months after she'd died, his sire had wed a younger lady who had tried her best to be a mother to her husband's three sons, but was more interested in her social engagements than parenting, even after giving birth to a daughter. Tristan's sire, however, had ensured that his children received the strict upbringing he'd envisioned for them.

As Cornelia tittered like a naughty girl, Tristan handed off his horse to a stable hand. The younger woman's gaze again traveled brazenly over him as he neared her and Radley, but he pretended not to have noticed.

"There you are," Radley said to him. "I will show you to your room."

"I will come with you." The younger woman hurried to keep up with their strides.

"No need." Radley said. "Why not wait with Mother and Honoria?"

"I can help you."

Help? What kind of aide did she think she could give two trained warriors? Refusing to acknowledge the bawdy thoughts that came to mind, Tristan said, "You are very kind, but I would like to wash before I go to the hall. I feel a bit grubby after my travels today, and I do want to be the perfect guest."

"You already are."

"Cornelia," Radley insisted, "you will wait in the hall."

She pouted. "I have hardly seen you in the past few days, since you have been busy with one matter or another. Also, Tristan's visit is the most exciting thing to have happened in weeks."

Tristan acknowledged a flare of sympathy. His half-sister had often complained about being born a noblewoman: the tiresome lessons in ladylike posture, needlework, etiquette, grooming, and household management that went on and on. She'd vowed she might die of sheer boredom. Of course, she hadn't; she was now married and expecting her first child. Mayhap once Cornelia had enjoyed their company for a bit, she'd be content to occupy herself elsewhere.

She was, after all, the daughter of a prominent lord who'd been of immense help to Radley. Tristan would be wise to ensure he didn't upset or disappoint her, not when he'd be introduced to Lord de Bretagne on the morrow.

As Tristan's career advanced, he might one day need to ask a favor of his lordship.

"We will not be too long upstairs," Tristan promised. "Once we join you in the hall, we will tell you of some of our adventures together. If you would like that, of course."

"Oh, I most certainly would."

Chapter Three

"Tristan has such aristocratic features," Lady Whitford said, once the forebuilding door had shut behind them.

"He does," Honoria agreed, while Willow raced up the stairwell to the great hall, no doubt heading for the hearth.

The air in the forebuilding smelled dank after the freshness of outside. Burning reed torches along the walls banished some but not all of the murky shadows as Honoria helped her mother up the uneven stone steps.

"I wonder if Tristan is married."

Honoria silently groaned. Not this conversation *again*.

For years, her mother had been trying to see her wed. Despite the numerous suitors who'd visited the castle and whom Honoria had met at tournaments, feasts, and other events, none had seemed quite right for her. That feeling of "rightness" was crucial; the knights and damsels in the old stories knew when they'd found their soul-mates, and that's what she aspired to, too.

"Did Radley mention if Tristan is wed or betrothed?" her mother pressed.

"He did not." Thankfully, there were only a few more steps until they reached the hall.

"I will try to find a way to ask."

"Please do not meddle. I do not need help finding a

husband."

"Honoria—"

"I will marry when I have found the right man." She would have added 'as Father agreed,' but it didn't seem fair to bring her deceased sire into the discussion just yet.

They reached the vast expanse of the hall. In the sunlight filtering in through the high, animal-horn-covered windows, Lady Whitford paused and studied Honoria—a look that still had the power to make Honoria feel five years old and inadequate.

Maidservants at the rows of oak trestle tables were setting out jugs of wine and ale in readiness for the evening meal. The table nearest the hearth was still heaped with the branches of evergreens, pine cones, twine, and red silk ribbon that Honoria had been using to decorate the hall.

Aware that her mother's gaze hadn't wavered, Honoria said quietly, "Father said I did not have to wed until I wished to."

"I remember. I only want what is best for you. I want you to *live*, to experience love, and not merely in the pages of your books."

Honoria *did* tend to escape into her tomes, but she simply couldn't help it. Her father had read some of the stories to her when she was a girl, and the tales kept his memory alive. When she read the words on the parchment pages, she heard her sire's voice and felt his arm around her as she snuggled in close.

A draft swept across the hall floor; someone had opened the outer door to the bailey.

Lady Whitford shivered. "Please, help me to the hearth. I need to sit by the fire."

"Of course." Honoria slid her arm around her mother's waist and guided her toward the blaze, where Willow was dozing.

"You have done a fine job of the decorating," her

ladyship murmured as she sank down into a carved oak chair. Firelight flickered on the evergreen boughs tied with clusters of pine cones and red ribbon bows that swept around the massive stone hearth. Honoria had also looped evergreens around most of the iron brackets holding the wall torches, and the piquant scents of pine and fir now lingered in the air.

Honoria smiled, for she was pleased with the decorations. Her father would have liked them, too—and would have hidden wrapped sweets amongst the evergreens for the servants' children to find and enjoy. "There is still more to do, but I am hoping Cornelia will help me."

Male voices echoed in the forebuilding, along with girlish laughter. Radley, Tristan, and Cornelia emerged into the hall. The men were carrying weapons and saddlebags. Cornelia was clearly trying to snare Tristan's attention.

He glanced over the hall and then found Honoria. Her body immediately recalled when their gazes had locked outside, and a peculiar heat whipped through her, a sensation akin to standing too close to the flames.

How annoying that he should affect her so.

She swiftly turned to pick up the fire poker and jab it in the blaze, dislodging one of the logs and stirring up a cloud of sparks.

"Careful, Sis," Radley said as they walked past. "You might set the garland alight."

Tristan tsked. "She might set *herself* alight."

Cornelia giggled.

"I am not a fool." Honoria hated that her cheeks grew hot. "I *have* tended a fire before." Keeping the fires going was one of the servants' tasks, but still, she'd added logs to the hearth in her chamber now and again, especially on freezing cold nights.

Tristan faced her. Regret touched his gaze as he said, "Forgive me. I did not mean any offense." He smiled in a most charming, boyish way, and she suddenly felt a bit lightheaded. "What I should have said is that 'twould be a shame if your costly garments were damaged by sparks, or if you suffered a burn on your fair skin."

"Oh." She hadn't realized he'd been concerned. She had indeed seen burn marks, caused by wayward sparks, on servants' clothes. "Well, you are most kind."

He nodded, an elegant dip of his dark head. "Damsels are to be protected, after all."

As Cornelia moved in to warm her hands at the fire, Tristan again fell in alongside Radley and they climbed the wooden stairs up to the landing overlooking the hall. They disappeared into the upper corridor leading to Radley's solar, the chambers belonging to the rest of the family, and the guest rooms.

"Well," Lady Whitford said with an astonished smile.

Honoria inwardly cringed. Knowing her mother, she was now convinced that Honoria and Tristan were going to be married by Christmas.

"That conversation meant naught, Mother," Honoria said firmly and returned the fire poker to its holder.

"Are you quite sure?"

"I am. He was only being chivalrous."

Crossing her arms, Cornelia studied the garland around the hearth. Yesterday, when asked to help with the decorating, the younger woman had set her hand to her brow and insisted the smell of evergreens was making her feel ill and that she needed some fresh air or she might swoon, leaving Honoria to work on her own while her mother rested upstairs.

Was Cornelia now going to find a flaw in the decorations to criticize?

Doing her best not to give in to annoyance, Honoria faced her parent. "Are you feeling warmer? Shall I ask the servants to bring some mulled wine?"

"'Twould be lovely," her mother said.

Cornelia sniffed, a disparaging sound, and gestured to the garland. "Where is the mistletoe, Honoria?"

"Mistletoe?"

The younger woman arched her eyebrows. "The greenery with white berries? The one that grows in the orchard's apple trees?"

"I *do* know what it looks like. I decided not to include it in the hearth decorations."

"We will need some to make the kissing bough." Cornelia straightened a ribbon bow. "Surely you are not waiting until Christmas Eve to gather the mistletoe? Few folk still heed the ancient custom that says it cannot be brought inside before then."

"We follow some of the old customs at Ellingstow, but not that one." Her ladyship chuckled. "Honoria's father enjoyed the fun of the kissing bough too much."

Honoria fought a pang of regret, for she remembered her sire, his eyes sparkling with mischief, stealing kisses from her mother under the kissing bough the Christmas before he'd died. "I had intended to gather mistletoe on the morrow," Honoria said.

"Why not today?" the younger woman asked.

"Well, because we just got home, and 'twill be getting dark soon."

Cornelia's attention shifted to the upstairs corridor. "Those two might be a while. We can pick it now."

"*Now?* But—"

"Do not be so disagreeable. 'Twill not take us long."

"You did not tell me Honoria is a beauty."

Radley, leaning in the doorway of the guest chamber,

seemed surprised. He shrugged. "She is my little sister."

Tristan set his saddlebag on the oak-framed bed in the small but spotlessly clean room. "So? You are a man. You have eyes."

Radley grinned. "I do, but I do not think of Sis in such a manner. She will always be the curious girl I taught how to catch grasshoppers, fish, and swim in the river before I was sent to Lincolnshire to train as a page."

An astonished laugh broke from Tristan. "Did you really teach her those things?"

"Aye. Being two years younger than I, she looked up to me. We had many adventures together."

Envy gnawed at Tristan as he unbuckled his bag, for Radley's affection for Honoria was clear in his voice. Tristan had never had that kind of relationship with his siblings. As far back as he could remember, he and his brothers had always competed against one another, to see who was best at shooting arrows, or fastest at rowing across the lake, or able to woo the prettiest castle maids. His father had encouraged their ambitions, vowing his sons would grow up to be among the most renowned and honorable knights in all of England—a measure by which every other accomplishment, large or small, was measured and judged. Tristan, destined to be his sire's heir, had been subject to especially rigorous expectations, and still was, as he'd learned during his last conversation with his father.

Mentally shoving aside stirred-up anger and regret, Tristan said, "Your sister seems too well-bred to have ever picked up grasshoppers."

"Aye, well, she changed as she grew up, especially after our parents became good friends with the de Bretagnes. When Cornelia moved here to be a ward of my sire, Sis felt responsible for her, as if Cornelia were her younger sister."

"I see."

Radley shook his head. "Honoria was also Father's

favorite. When he was brought here, near dead after the ambush, she refused to leave his side. In his herbal, she found recipes for poultices and ointments that she showed to the healer, and together, they worked day and night to try and save him. Honoria was determined that he was going to live. When he died, 'twas as if something inside her shattered. She was devastated."

Tristan's gaze dropped to the bed. He knew all too well the anguish of losing a beloved parent. "I am sorry about your sire."

"I strive every day to rule Ellingstow as well as he did." Radley's expression turned thoughtful. "I know your relationship with your brothers is strained after what happened with Odelia. But, if friendship is what all of you want...?"

"Mayhap." Tristan reached into his bag for clean garments and set them on the coverlet. "Such matters can wait until after the holidays." By then his sire's anger might have cooled somewhat. "Right now, I want to make merry and enjoy the season to the fullest."

"An excellent plan. Yet, tell me, why are you so interested in Honoria? Do you wish to court her? I thought you had sworn off relationships."

"True, I—"

"Knowing you, you are more interested in Cornelia."

He was certainly *not* tempted by the younger lady.

Before Tristan could answer, Radley stepped inside the chamber and shut the door. Crossing to the bed, he said quietly, "I might as well tell you now. I was going to tell you anyway."

Radley sounded terribly grave. "Please do not say you have suddenly decided to forsake all earthly pleasures, including excessive drinking and rowdy singing."

"I am not going to do that," Radley said, laughing.

"Thank God."

"'Tis an unfortunate circumstance I must reveal to you. However, I trust 'twill make Cornelia's brazenness a little more understandable."

Tristan was well-experienced with the fairer sex and knew what a woman wanted when she flirted with him. Yet, Cornelia was a gently-raised young lady. She'd surely been taught that bold flirtation wasn't appropriate for a woman of her refined lineage.

Did she act the way she did out of defiance, then?

"It happened about two years ago," Radley said.

It happened. An event, then. Some kind of tragedy?

"Cornelia, her mother, and older brother were traveling to a town several leagues away when a bad storm hit. The road became slick with rainwater and mud and their carriage capsized. It rolled down a slope and hit trees."

"God's blood," Tristan murmured. "Was anyone hurt?"

"The carriage driver survived, but not the guards. Cornelia's mother and sibling also perished. Cornelia hit her head in the accident and was rendered unconscious. While she recovered well enough, apart from a mark on her cheek, she has never quite been the same. The accident…changed her."

"How tragic," Tristan said. "Poor girl."

"While her scar is hardly noticeable to others, Cornelia frets about it constantly. She fears it makes her less appealing to suitors. Hence, her boldness."

Tristan shook his head. The young woman had no reason to worry. "She is young, pretty, and her sire is rich. She will not have trouble finding a husband."

"As I have told her. Her father has said such as well." Radley sighed. "His lordship, of course, suffers guilt over what happened to his wife and heir. Cornelia is the only family he has left, which explains why he has spoiled her."

"Spoiled?" Tristan said dryly. "I had not noticed."

Radley chuckled, before he again sobered. "His lordship finally acknowledged he needed help with Cornelia, and my father agreed she could live here as his ward. They both believed that Honoria would be a good influence on her."

"'Tis a lot of responsibility to place upon your sister."

"Aye, especially when Father died unexpectedly. Yet, I vow his death helped her form a strong bond with Cornelia; they share the pain of loss. Because of that bond, Sis tolerates Cornelia, even when she is mean."

Radley's sister was beginning to sound worthy of sainthood.

"Keep in mind what I have told you when dealing with Cornelia, all right?" Radley asked.

"I will."

"You are also not to repeat one word of what I said."

"I swear, as a knight of honor, I would never betray your confidence."

"Good." Radley strode to the doorway. "When you are ready, knock on my chamber door, and we will go down to the great hall together."

Chapter Four

S tanding on the leaf-strewn ground beside Cornelia, Honoria peered up at the steward at the top of the ladder, a basket slung over his left arm. She would have loved to gather the mistletoe from the apple tree herself, but Sydney, who had served their family for over thirty years, had insisted he be the one to climb the ladder, for he'd never forgive himself if his lord's sister fell and broke an arm or leg days before Christmas.

"Can you cut that bunch to the right?" she called to him.

Sydney pointed with his dagger to a cluster of white berries. "This one, milady?"

Cornelia hugged herself as the cold breeze whistled through the orchard. "How long is he going to take?" she muttered.

"Hush," Honoria answered. 'Twas shameful how rude Cornelia could be. "You were the one who insisted we pick mistletoe today." As the steward pointed to another bunch, seeking her approval, she said, "Closer to the fork in the branch…. Aye, there."

Leaning sideways, Sydney angled the knife.

The ladder wobbled. Honoria clutched it with both hands. She certainly didn't want Sydney to tumble to the ground. He'd be hurt, with so many tree roots having pushed up through the soil.

The steward didn't seem worried, though. With a leafy rustle, the cutting dropped down onto the branch near his waist, and he gathered several more bunches before putting them into the basket.

They would need plenty of mistletoe if they were to honor the tradition of plucking a berry from the kissing bough each time a kiss was stolen under it. No woman wanted to find herself under the kissing bough without a berry to be picked. She also mustn't refuse a kiss under the bough; if she did, according to lore, she wouldn't marry within the next year.

A tremor wove through Honoria, for what if Tristan happened to catch her under the kissing bough? She'd have to kiss him, a thoroughly exciting but daunting prospect.

"We must have plenty of mistletoe by now," Cornelia said, as the breeze gusted again.

"Aye." Honoria motioned for Sydney to come down.

"Look," the younger woman shrilled, "'Tis Radley and Tristan."

Honoria caught sight of the men walking toward them and sucked in a fortifying breath. She was not going to let Tristan unsettle her again. She was a grown woman, after all, not a young girl prone to infatuation.

Sydney stepped down from the ladder and handed her the filled basket, just as the men approached.

"Milords." The steward bowed.

"Good afternoon, Sydney," Radley said.

"What are you two doing in the garden?" Cornelia asked with a coy grin. "Did you miss us? Or did you want to get your hands on some mistletoe so you can kiss us witless?"

Honoria choked down a mortified groan. Did Cornelia ever think before she spoke?

Tristan's gaze sharpened, but Radley didn't seem bothered by the younger woman's questions. "Mother told us you were gathering mistletoe. We thought we would come and help, since I need to speak with Sydney anyway."

Honoria shivered as the wind gusted again.

"Are you all right?" Tristan asked her. "Would you like my cloak?"

What would it be like to slip on the garment warmed by his body? The wool would smell of the outdoors, leather, soap, and…him. She'd be enveloped in his essence, as if he'd wrapped his strong arms around her.

The skin across her bosom suddenly felt tight and hot, sensations she hadn't experienced before and must ponder once she was alone in her room. "I-I am heading inside shortly, but thank you for the offer."

"My pleasure."

Cornelia brushed up against him like a cat seeking attention. "I am cold, too."

"I am sure you are," he said with a wry grin.

Tristan reached to unfasten his cloak pin, and Honoria tightened her grip on the basket. She was not going to stay to witness Cornelia's antics. "Thank you for your help, Sydney. I am going to return to the keep." To the others, she said, "I will see you inside."

She walked away, leaves crunching under her boots.

Radley's voice followed her. "Cornelia, Tristan must keep his cloak, or he will catch a chill and be ill for Christmas."

"But—"

"Please go with Honoria. As soon as I have spoken with Sydney, Tristan and I will come inside."

Honoria reached the stone path leading to the garden gate, just as Cornelia caught up with her. The younger woman's face glowed. "Was that not most kind of Tristan to offer us his cloak?"

"Aye." He was only being gallant; surely Cornelia understood that.

The younger woman sighed happily. "Now that we have mistletoe, we can ensure we get plenty of kisses from him."

Honoria's gaze strayed to the greenery, rustling slightly in the basket as she walked. What was she going to do if Tristan drew her under the kissing bough, picked a berry, and wanted a kiss? Not a quick one on the cheek, as she was accustomed to giving, but one on the lips? What would she do then?

She'd never kissed a man on the mouth and had no idea what to do. Was the pressing together of lips gentle and tender, or hard and impassioned? What if she decided on a gentle kiss and Tristan expected more? What if she unintentionally offended him? Her innards clenched with dread, for if he kissed her, he'd know right away that she was inexperienced.

Could she practice kissing, so she'd be prepared? She had cloth dolls of a knight and a lady in her linen chest that she'd played with as a child.

Nay. She was *not* kissing a toy. Instead, she'd consult the book of romantic tales. Knights and ladies kissed in the stories; while she couldn't remember reading much detail about those kisses, she'd investigate as soon as she could.

Reaching the gate, she lifted the latch and she and Cornelia stepped through. The gate shut behind them with a *click*. "I cannot wait to kiss Tristan," the younger woman said. "He will make the perfect husband."

A surprised laugh broke from Honoria. "You hardly know him."

"He *is* a close friend of Radley's. That says a lot about Tristan's character."

"True, but—"

"We must make the kissing bough tonight." Cornelia's smile turned sly. "The sooner I kiss Tristan, the sooner he and I will be wed."

"You wanted to see me, Sydney?"

At Radley's question, Tristan tore his gaze from Honoria. She moved with such elegance, 'twas a pleasure to watch her. Yet, he didn't want to be caught ogling.

"Did the sheriff send some news of the investigation into my father's killing?" Radley asked.

"Nay, milord," the steward said. "Regrettably not."

Radley exhaled a harsh breath. "One day soon, I hope the sheriff will tell me that the attackers have been identified and arrested."

An intense pang of sympathy wove through Tristan. He couldn't imagine losing a parent the way Radley had.

"I wish for their capture too, milord," Sydney said. "Your sire was a fine man who did not deserve to die in such a ruthless manner. What I wanted to discuss, however, was what happened not long ago in the bailey. The captain of the guard will likely speak to you about it, but I felt you should be alerted as soon as possible."

Radley frowned. "Go on."

"Three men arrived on horseback. They were not tenants bringing rents. Two of them rode into the bailey, while the third did not cross the drawbridge, but waited a fair distance away. When guards questioned the two riders, they claimed to be travelers, going to visit friends for Christmas. They wanted directions to the next town, saying they had taken a wrong turn."

"You did not believe them?"

Brushing a mistletoe leaf from his cloak sleeve, Sydney said, "Few folk get lost in this area. Also, they lingered, as though assessing the castle's defenses."

Misgiving rippled through Tristan. "Did you get a

good look at these travelers?"

"I did not, milord. I was assisting a farmer who had brought his rents, so I did not speak to the riders myself. I do recall that they wore hooded cloaks that shielded their faces, but that is common at this time of year." Sydney shook his head. "I may be suspicious for no good reason—"

"But your instincts are usually sound," Radley cut in. "There is much discontent in England right now. Honorable men are being corrupted by promises of wealth and power if they will rebel against King John and the lords who support him. We must be alert to any potential threats to this keep."

"I agree," Sydney said. "'Tis why I wanted you to be aware of the incident, especially after what happened to your sire."

"Tell the guards who questioned the travelers that I wish to speak to them."

"Aye, milord." Sydney bowed and then folded up the ladder and carried it away.

"I wonder who those men were," Radley murmured as they started toward the keep.

"As do I." Tristan's foreboding burrowed deeper. His gut instincts were telling him that the rider who had stayed back from the fortress, the one unwilling to risk being recognized, was the man with the scarred face.

Chapter Five

"Your sister is fascinated by that book," Tristan said, sipping his wine. Honoria was sitting by the fire, poring over a tome propped up in her lap—a different one than she'd purchased at the market. The wolfhound named Willow lay asleep at her feet. Several more tomes rested on the oak table beside Honoria.

She'd joined Tristan, Radley, Lady Whitford, and Cornelia for the evening repast, but as soon as the meal had ended, she'd rushed to the hearth and become engrossed in her book. She was frowning, which suggested that what she was reading was important.

Seated beside Tristan at the lord's table on the stone dais, Radley poured them both more wine from a silver jug. "Father often read to Sis and me when we were children. Honoria loved the stories, and once Father taught her to read, there was no end to her interest in books. She inherited all but the one she bought today from him," Radley said, before downing some of the piquant red.

"I see." Tristan struggled to suppress the memory of his father throwing leather-bound tomes against the wall, parchment pages breaking loose and drifting down to the floor while he ranted that Tristan's reading was a waste of effort that should be spent honing his fighting prowess. Words didn't win battles, his sire had railed; weapons did.

"My sire believed one could learn a lot from books,"

Radley added, "if one chose to heed the wisdom written down by those who have lived before us."

"He was a wise man."

"Aye." Radley's tone roughened. "I miss him, as does Honoria. I vow she may never recover from his death."

Tristan fingered a drop of wine from the stem of his goblet as he glanced at her again, and then across the large chamber. Apart from Honoria, the hall with its rush-strewn floor and large tapestries depicting scenes from historic battles was empty of all but a few young children sleeping on pallets in the far corner, with mongrels curled up beside them. The trestle tables used by the castle folk for the meal had been folded and stacked along the walls. The servants were away completing their evening chores, but would soon be returning to the hall to lay down their pallets and sleep.

While folk had cleared up after the meal, Tristan and Radley had talked with Cornelia and Lady Whitford. Her ladyship had soon retired to her bedchamber, and not long after, Cornelia had grown weary of the conversation. With enough drama to make her the lead in a Christmas pantomime, she'd excused herself and gone upstairs to fetch materials needed to make a kissing bough. "What an exciting time we will have when 'tis done," she'd said.

Tristan hadn't responded. He wasn't going to encourage her; not if she intended to use the kissing bough in the manner he expected.

The *pop* of a burning log drew his attention back to the hearth. Fire glow cast golden light over Honoria sitting with her head slightly bowed, her braided hair pulled over one shoulder. The plait skimmed the swell of her breast and ended somewhere near her lap. He suddenly had the wild desire to loosen her hair, to feel the silken strands against his fingers, and to allow more of her tresses to be gilded by firelight.

He forced the urge aside. Such intimacy between a

man and woman implied more than friendship, and he *wasn't* interested in courting Honoria or any other lady.

As Honoria turned a page in the tome, her frown deepened. What *was* she reading? He'd love to know.

Beside him, Radley set his goblet down and peered into the wine jug. "'Tis almost empty, and the night's drinking has only just begun."

"Hellfire." Tristan did his best to appear miffed. He well knew Radley wouldn't let them run out of wine.

"I will fetch more from the cellar. 'Twill be quicker than summoning a servant."

"I will come with you."

"No need. I will not be long. Just stay out of trouble while I am away, all right?" Radley grinned, rose with the scrape of his chair, and headed for the antechamber off the hall.

Silence spread through the room. Honoria hadn't moved from the hearth and seemed oblivious to the fact that Tristan was still sitting at the table. She *had* to know he was there, though.

Tristan sipped his drink, unable to ignore a rising sense of disgruntlement. Her indifference no doubt bothered him more than it should because he'd drunk plenty of wine tonight. Yet, foolish as 'twas, he couldn't help feeling slighted. Was he losing his charm with the ladies? He'd never been ignored before. Ever.

'Twas damned...perplexing. And aggravating.

Enough.

He set down his goblet, stood, and crossed to the hearth. Honoria was, after all, his best friend's sister. There was no harm in deepening their friendship.

As he neared, she looked up from the book.

Tristan gestured to the chair beside her. "May I join you?"

Her fingers curled tighter on the tome's leather cover,

as though she was reluctant to agree. Yet, she nodded. "If you wish."

He sat; the chair creaked as he leaned back, folded his arms, and stretched his legs out toward the blaze, being careful not to hit Willow who had stirred at his approach. Head raised, her front paws on the hearth tiles, the wolfhound studied him intently, as though assessing whether he was worthy of being so close to Honoria.

"What are you reading?" Tristan asked.

"Old folk tales."

"They must be good stories…or rather sinful ones."

Honoria looked startled. "Why do you say that?"

"You have hardly glanced up from that book."

A pretty blush reddened her face. "The tales are not that bawdy."

Nay? Why was she blushing, then? Resisting the impulse to point that out to her, he merely said, "If you say so."

"I do. I would not read such stories. Even if I did, I would not read them in the hall."

He savored the spark in her eyes. Teasing her was at least getting her attention.

"I often read after the evening meal," she insisted. "It helps my mind settle for sleep."

Reading before falling asleep sounded like an excellent idea. Tristan could have used such a tactic during the past weeks, when his disagreement with his sire had kept him awake more nights than he cared to admit. "I must try that sometime," he said. "Unfortunately, I do not have any books to read now."

She closed the tome and set it on her lap. "You said 'now.' Did you have books before?"

Memories crowded into Tristan's mind, and he couldn't keep his voice from hardening. "I did once, but my father destroyed them."

"*Destroyed* them?" She sounded appalled.

"My sire expected his sons to grow up to be famous warriors. He believed that if we had any free moments, we should spend them practicing swordplay, or archery, or fighting opponents in the tiltyards. To sit and read was akin to being idle."

Sadness registered in her eyes. "I am guessing your father found you reading one day?"

"He did." Tristan uncrossed his arms and leaned forward to brace his elbows on his knees. Heat from the fire warmed his fingers. "To be honest, I never wanted to be a knight. I longed to be a scholar."

"Truly?" she asked.

"Mmm. As I grew up, I wanted to know more about the world around me. The dates, saffron, and cumin that our cook used in special recipes, for example. They were not from England, but brought here on ships that docked in London. What was it like, traveling on the ocean? What did folk pack for such a journey? Were the stars in the heavens as bright over the sea as the ones over my father's keep?"

"I have often pondered such questions," she said, her words warm with excitement. Now he definitely had her full attention.

"One afternoon, while I was in the local village having the handle of my dagger repaired, I went into a shop and found two dust-covered books," Tristan continued. "They cost all of my spending money, but they were worth the price to me. One contained the personal writings of a lord who had died nigh thirty years ago. The shopkeeper told me that when King John had seized the keep from the lord's rebellious heir, almost all of the possessions had been sold off to pay outstanding debts. The items considered to be of little value ended up in the shopkeeper's premises."

"The tome was considered to be of little worth?"

"Regrettably, aye. Another of the books contained

chansons and unfinished compositions. I wondered if the musician had lived in the same castle as the lord."

"What marvelous finds," she mused.

"They were indeed. When my father found me reading them, though, he was furious. I had skipped archery practice with my brothers so I could read. I apologized and pleaded with my sire, but he grabbed the books from my hands and threw them against the wall. He broke the covers. Parchment pages went everywhere."

"Nay!"

"I am afraid so. My father vowed that if he caught me with a book again, I would suffer a far worse punishment. My sire was—*is*—not a man to be crossed." Tristan looked down at his hands. "To this day, I have not bought another tome."

"What happened to the ones you had purchased?"

"I gathered up the loose pages, but had no idea how to restore the books. I knew that if I tried to hire someone to fix them, my father would find out, and he'd view my actions as disobedience."

"Oh, Tristan."

"In the end I threw the lot into the bottom of my linen chest. I had forgotten about those tomes until tonight."

Rustling fabric drew his gaze to her. She offered him her book. "Would you like to see it?"

"I would indeed."

The coolness of the leather against his palms sent a thrill of anticipation rippling down his spine. The book was beautiful. Its cover bore an intricate design of Celtic knotwork. As he opened the tome to read the title page penned in a flourish of black ink, the scent of cured parchment greeted him.

As she'd said, 'twas a book of ancient stories. *Romantic* ones passed down through the ages. A chuckle welled within him, for he hadn't been so wrong, then, about sinful stories.

Raising his brows, he looked at her.

"Why are you gazing at me so? Do you not like the title?"

"The title is exactly what I expected."

"Folk tales—"

"*Romantic* tales."

She folded her arms across her bosom.

He made a valiant effort not to ogle her luscious breasts brimming above her arms; he focused instead on the early pages of the tome.

"Romantic stories are favored by noblemen and ladies alike," she said, as though needing to justify what she'd been reading. "Some of the most famous *chansons de geste,* sung in halls all across England, are romances."

"So they may be." Tristan turned more pages. The craftsmanship of the lettering was exceptional. "Tristan and Iseult," he said, finding his given name in the tome. "You do not find their tale scandalous? She was promised to his uncle, but Tristan, renowned as a most chivalrous knight, took her as his lover anyway."

"They were hardly to blame. They did not know that the potion they drank was magical, and that 'twould make them fall deeply in love."

He turned more pages. "Arthur and Guinevere, then. 'Tis rather wicked how Guinevere loved Lancelot when she was married to Arthur, aye?"

"I suppose." Frowning, Honoria added, "Where did you learn about the ancient stories? Not from books, I am guessing."

He shook his head. "Most I heard when I was training with your brother in Lincolnshire. In the garrison in the evenings, the men-at-arms liked to tell stories." Pointing to the tome's thick spine, he asked, "Have you read all of this book?"

"Aye, several times."

So she enjoyed the legends enough to re-read them. There were tame versions of the stories, though, and there were lewd ones. How he longed to know how passionate hers were. "Tell me, in this book, do the lords and ladies hold hands?"

"Aye."

"Do knights rescue damsels and win their undying love?"

"There is plenty of courtship."

"And…do they kiss?"

Honoria went very still. Her blush returned.

"No kissing?" he pressed. There *had* to be kissing. No knight in his right mind would ever miss the chance to kiss a beautiful damsel.

"Some of the tales…do involve kissing." Her last words were almost a squeak.

And do they couple? The words were on the tip of his tongue when footfalls sounded on the landing: Cornelia was returning.

Her strides slowed when she saw him sitting by the fire. Her features hardened, but then she continued at a brisk pace to the staircase down to the hall.

Honoria scooted to the edge of her chair. From her stack of books, she took the one she'd purchased that day. The wolfhound pushed up to standing and stretched.

"I must help Cornelia now." Honoria seemed most eager to flee.

"Of course." He'd tormented her enough about her book and kissing for one day.

"When you have finished looking at the tome, please put it with the others."

In the torch-lit antechamber off the hall, servants had cleared serving platters and wine jugs from the table to make room for the basket of mistletoe and other gathered items that Honoria was using for decorating. She went to the table to set down the book. Willow padded along at her side and flopped down near the wall, where she could watch what was going on while washing her front paws.

Hands on her hips, Cornelia faced Honoria. "What were you doing?" she whispered fiercely.

"What do you mean?" She'd never seen the younger woman quite so flushed and angry.

Cornelia thrust a finger in Honoria's face. "You were sitting with Tristan. *Alone.*"

"Not completely alone. Children are sleeping—"

"You know what I mean."

"Radley was only going to be gone for a moment," she said in hushed tones, hoping their discussion wouldn't carry to Tristan. "Since Tristan and I were the only ones in the hall—"

"He is *mine*. Remember?"

An uncomfortable ache spread through Honoria. Not jealousy. Surely not.

The flickering wall torch nearby illuminated the hard set of Cornelia's jaw. "I told you earlier, Honoria. I said he and I would wed."

"You did indeed. Should you not consult Tristan, though, regarding your plans to marry him?"

"My father is a rich and high-ranking lord," Cornelia bit out. "Tristan will gain new allies and opportunities by marrying me. I am also young, beautiful, and willing to bear him many sons. Why would he not want me?"

All that Cornelia had said was true. Yet, love was an integral part of marriage, was it not? 'Twas for most of the lords and ladies in the old tales, and it certainly had been for Honoria's parents.

"Cornelia, please consider—"

"I have. He is the one I want."

"So he may be, but does he *care* for you?" Honoria asked softly. "Does he make you laugh, share your dreams, know your secrets, make you feel giddy with happiness—"

The younger woman rolled her eyes. "You have been reading your stupid books again."

"They are not stupid." Determined to remain calm, Honoria added, "Marriage is not a commitment to enter lightly."

"Some ladies have no choice at all in whom they marry. Remember that fourteen-year-old noblewoman we met last year, who had received word from the crown that she was to wed a lord she had never met? The man was more than thirty years her senior."

Honoria shuddered, for she remembered that resigned young lady very well. For days afterward, she and Cornelia had talked about the horrors of marrying a stranger, one who was old enough to have been their father.

"Your sire has enough influence with the crown that you will never have to face such a situation," Honoria said. "That means you have a choice in the man who will be your husband."

"I have chosen Tristan."

Honoria sighed. While the younger woman strained her patience sometimes, Honoria truly wanted her friend to be happy. Cornelia had bravely endured the loss of her mother and brother, and deserved to be wed to someone who would cherish her. There were lots of other lords in England who might be better suited to her. "Be honest, Cornelia. Does Tristan—"

"Does he love me?" The younger woman snorted. "I will make him fall in love." She gestured to the costly ribbons she'd dropped on the table. "With our kissing bough, I will win him over. I will be the only lady he desires."

Honoria eyed the ribbons. They were ordinary silk, not wrought from some divine fabric that could bring about miracles. How did she stop Cornelia from rushing into what could be a terrible mistake?

"Do not say another word," the younger lady muttered. "I do not wish to discuss the matter anymore. Now, you will help me with the kissing bough. Get that useless book out of the way, will you?"

'Twas not a useless book, as Cornelia would soon realize. "I brought it to show you something inside."

"All right, but be quick about it."

Honoria opened the tome and thumbed through it until she found the page she sought. She spread the book flat so both she and Cornelia could see.

The younger woman wrinkled her nose. "The parchment smells."

"The scent is not so unpleasant." Pointing to the drawing of a ball of evergreens and mistletoe woven through with ribbons and tied with bows, Honoria said, "Shall we make one like this? 'Tis a little more elaborate than usual."

Cornelia sniffed. "Fine."

"Good. Help me tie some evergreen branches into a round shape."

While they worked, Radley, carrying a small wine cask, emerged from the stairwell that led up from the cellar and storage chambers. Seeing them, he lurched to a halt, clearly wavering on his feet from too much drink.

"All is well?" he asked.

Before Honoria could utter a word, Cornelia said, "Go away, please. You are not allowed to see the kissing bough until 'tis finished."

Chapter Six

Tristan lifted his gaze from the book as Radley approached, carrying the silver jug and goblets he'd collected from the lord's table. Upon returning from the cellar, Radley had filled the jug with wine from the cask he'd fetched.

Judging by his unsteady strides, Radley was a right drunken sot. Tristan wasn't clear-headed himself. Sluggish heat ran in his veins and muddied his thoughts. He wasn't as inebriated as Radley, but years of drinking with his mates had taught him he'd be a fool to get on a horse now and race into battle or challenge a rival to a swordfight. He'd never had to face the former situation, but the latter…. He had the scars to remind him of the duel he'd fought with one of his brothers while they'd both been angry and drunk. Luckily neither of them had ended up badly wounded.

Radley set down what he carried and dropped into the chair Honoria had recently vacated. "I have grave news, my friend."

Parchment rustled as Tristan turned to the next page in the tome. "Really? What news?"

"Honoria and Cornelia are plotting."

"Cornelia certainly is." Despite his proximity to the fire, Tristan had heard the women talking in hushed tones. Cornelia's voice had been the most forceful, although he hadn't been able to make out a word she'd said. He might regret that later.

Pouring wine into the goblets, Radley said, "We surely can thwart any mischief those two might design."

"I would hope so, but we should not underestimate them. According to the stories in this book, beautiful women can be a man's downfall. They can also be his redemption."

Leaning in, Radley squinted at the tome. "Ah, I recognize that one. 'Twas Father's favorite."

"'Tis quite a collection: Stories about love, honor, and passion."

Radley grunted.

"Apparently, some of the tales involve kissing."

"Kissing? You mean men and women pressing their mouths together and enjoying it?" Radley feigned shock. "How could my little sister be reading such things?"

"She got rather flustered when we were discussing the stories." Curiosity gnawed at Tristan, and while he tried to squash the unwise emotion, the drink overruled his better judgment. "Has Honoria ever been kissed by a man?"

Radley shrugged; he banged his elbow on the chair arm and winced. "How would I know?"

"She might have confided in you."

"She and I are close, but she would have talked to Mother or Cornelia about such matters."

Disappointment wove through Tristan. He shouldn't care whether Honoria had experienced such intimacy before. Still, the curiosity in him wouldn't be silenced.

"If you want my brotherly opinion, though, I would guess she has not."

A ridiculous flare of triumph warmed Tristan. "What makes you say that?"

"She has never really been interested in courting, certainly not since Father's death. Father agreed she would not have to marry until she was ready, and I guess she has not met the right lord yet."

"She wants to find true love."

"Do not we all?"

Tristan had learned the hard way that unless a man and woman loved one another equally, and were committed to sustaining that love, their romance was doomed. But, he knew enough happily-married couples to know true love was attainable and desirable.

Radley drank some wine. "Cornelia, however…."

"Aye?"

"I know she has been kissed on the lips, because…well…I kissed her."

"*You* did?"

Radley nodded. "We were all going to a feast, not long after Father died. I was overwhelmed with all of my new duties, and she looked so lovely, and I…could not resist." He smiled sheepishly and stared down into his wine. "No one else was around, so no one else knows. She laughed afterward, as though the kiss meant naught, but to me…."

Radley sounded like a man who was smitten. As swiftly as the emotion had entered his voice, however, it vanished on rough laughter. "I do not know why I told you that."

"Nor do I, but you hardly did aught wrong. You are lord and master of this keep. If you want to kiss Cornelia, 'tis your right."

"Aye, well, we both know that men of our position have to be careful. She could have told Mother, her sire, and the rest of the castle folk about our kiss. I would have been obliged to propose to her."

"You are lucky, then, that she kept quiet."

"I suppose."

Surely that wasn't a hint of regret in Radley's voice?

Tristan glanced down at the tome, and a word on the page caught his eye. He chuckled.

"You found something amusing?"

Tristan set his finger on the particular line and read: "'Her bountiful lips were the vibrant red of polished rubies. Her eyes, as blue as a cloudless summer sky, glowed with the tremendous love gathered in her breast.'"

"Breast?" Radley waggled his eyebrows. "The right one or the left?"

"I will have to read on to find out."

"The Lady of the Glowing Breast." Radley raised his goblet in a toast. "A woman so remarkable, she is a legend."

Tristan laughed. "At least in the middle of the night, her lover can easily find her."

"He looks for the glow."

Tristan snickered, and Radley chortled. Soon, the hall echoed with their laughter.

"Whatever are they finding so amusing?" Cornelia asked while she tied mistletoe to the kissing bough.

"No doubt Radley has told a bawdy jest." Honoria adjusted part of the ribbon shot through with gold thread. Their project was coming together beautifully.

"Tristan was likely the one to tell the jest," the younger woman countered. "I expect he knows plenty of them."

Honoria was growing quite weary of Tristan being the focus of every conversation.

She finished securing the ribbon, but before she could give it one last tweak, Cornelia yanked the kissing bough toward her and picked it up by the ribbon loop at the top. "I say 'tis done. Shall we go show it to the men?"

And watch Cornelia trap Tristan into kissing her? *Ugh.*

Honoria gathered up some loose berries. "I will tidy up here."

"The servants will clean up this mess." The younger woman headed for the archway that led into the hall. "Come on."

Honoria would much rather go to her bedchamber and read the gloriously thrilling old stories. Yet, as Cornelia disappeared from view, and the quietude of the antechamber wrapped around Honoria, she realized she *had* to follow. She'd left her books in the hall.

As though sensing her reluctance, Willow stood, her tail wagging in encouragement. "I know," Honoria said. "The sooner I get the tomes, the sooner we can read together." Every night, the hound stretched out on the bed beside Honoria; sometimes Honoria even read exciting passages aloud, which Willow seemed to enjoy.

Indignant cries and laughter drifted in from the hall. Resolving to say goodnight as swiftly as possible, Honoria picked up the tome containing the kissing bough drawing and went to join the others…and gasped.

Cornelia stood giggling near the men. Radley, grinning and leaning so far over he was falling out of his chair, was holding onto a corner of the book of tales.

Tristan swatted at his hand while tugging the tome toward him.

They were going to ruin it!

"I am lord of this keep," Radley griped, laughing. "Let me see."

"I read the words exactly, *milord*," Tristan answered.

Willow barked.

Radley tugged again on the tome.

"Let go." Chuckling, Tristan swatted again.

Bark, bark.

"Cease!" Honoria marched to stand in front of her brother. "You are going to tear my book. *Father*'s book." The anguish of their sire's passing stirred anew, along with a reminder of the promise she'd made, her fingers linked through his as he lay dying: to take care of his prized books.

"Sis, I swear, I would never—"

"You cannot make such a promise. 'Tis easily done by accident, especially when drunk."

Her brother slumped back in his chair.

She glared at Tristan. His stare didn't waver. Disquiet sifted through her, and she nudged her chin higher, refusing to heed the urge to look away. She held out her free hand in a silent demand for the book.

Tristan's gaze traveled over her fingers, spread open like a wild rose. Her skin, the center of her palm, grew warm, as if he'd touched her.

She trembled, but remained steadfast.

He closed the tome and set it on his lap.

Oh, the wretched rogue.

"Please give me back my book."

"I will," Tristan said. "Radley spoke true, though. We intended no harm to your tome. We were merely jesting."

"You mean, mocking what you were reading."

"Some of the descriptions *are* rather fanciful."

"I thought you would appreciate the ancient tales," she continued, unable to slow the indignant words. "I thought you understood how special my books are to me."

"I did," Tristan said. "I do. We—"

"I would like my book back. *Now.*"

His jaw clenched. He obviously didn't want to concede to her demand.

Willow growled. Honoria stroked the dog's back to try and calm her.

"Do not be so upset, Honoria," Cornelia said. "Your tome is fine." Moving closer, she held up the kissing bough. "Now, look what we—"

"The book," Honoria repeated, proud her voice

didn't falter.

"Better give it back, Tris," Radley said.

"Very well." Tristan picked it up and held it out to her. Her fingers closed on it, but he didn't immediately relinquish it to her. "I swear to you, on my honor, that I would not have let any harm come to your book."

Honoria pulled it toward her. This time, Tristan let go.

She snatched up the rest of her books and walked away.

"That did not go at all as I had planned," Tristan said.

He dragged his hand over his mouth as Honoria and her loyal hound disappeared into the corridor leading off the landing. He hadn't been able to wrest his gaze from her as she'd climbed the stairs, her gown swaying with each of her strides, her hair gleaming like polished metal. She was so very beautiful, even when furious.

Radley rubbed his brow and stared into his goblet. Neither of them had intended offense. Aye, matters had gotten a bit out of hand, but he and Radley were chivalrous men, sworn to cherish the fairer sex and all that was important to them.

He must set matters right with Honoria, and not only to ensure a pleasant Christmas for all. 'Twas a matter of honor.

As though attuned to Tristan's thoughts, Radley said, "Honoria will be all right once she has calmed down."

"I hope so. Should I go after her?"

"Nay," Cornelia said.

"And do what?" Radley asked at the same time.

"Apologize, for a start."

Radley shook his head. "You tried that, remember? She would not listen."

"I am willing to try again."

Setting down his drink, Radley said, "Knowing my sister, she will refuse to open her chamber door to speak to you. She will tell you to go away."

"I am prepared to face such obstacles." Indeed, as a knight, Tristan was obliged to do whatever must be done to succeed in a quest.

"Honestly, Tris, I would wait until morning. My sister might be ready to listen then."

"I agree, 'tis the best plan." Cornelia sidled closer. "While Honoria might have left for the night, there is no reason why we cannot enjoy ourselves." With a mischievous grin, she swung the kissing bough from side to side, as though weighing which one of them she'd kiss first.

Tristan frowned, for her flirtations were wasted on him. He couldn't forget the challenge blazing in Honoria's eyes, and how she'd not yielded to his stare. She had a warrior's spirit; the resolve of the famous heroines in her tales. *That* was the kind of woman with whom he'd willingly share a kiss.

Just then, women's voices carried from the forebuilding. Servants were returning to the hall to bed down for the night.

"Before we hang this over the entrance to the hall, we need to try it out," Cornelia said. "Which one of you rogues is going to kiss me, or shall *I* choose?"

Radley had been right about needing to beware. A kiss on the lips between a lord and a lady in front of witnesses—including servants—could be interpreted as a promise of courtship, or even betrothal. He didn't know Cornelia well, but he sure didn't trust her; not when her sire's influence could advance or destroy a nobleman's career.

Cornelia could easily turn her face at the last instant and make what was meant to be a kiss on the cheek into one on the mouth. *That* was a trick he'd expect from Odelia, and by God, he was not going to let a woman manipulate him ever again.

Tristan set his hands on the arms of the chair to rise, but the younger woman lunged to stand in front of him. She raised the bough, clearly readying to hold it over his head and steal a kiss.

Rebellion sparked like hot fire within him. He shoved back his chair and stood, thwarting Cornelia's trickery.

Disappointment filled her gaze. He offered an apologetic smile to soften the sting of his refusal. "I just remembered I must go and check on my horse."

Cornelia huffed. "But—"

Radley caught her free hand. "Will you sit with me while I finish my wine? I hate to drink alone."

She answered, but Tristan was already across the hall and loping down the forebuilding stairs, passing three maidservants on the way. While he wasn't keen on abandoning his friend to Cornelia, Radley obviously knew how to handle her. Tristan did need to check on his destrier, as well as calm his mind. The night air would help purge his annoyance.

He stepped out into the dark bailey and headed for the stable. The breeze held a forewarning of overnight frost as it nipped at his face and hands.

The sweetish scents of horses and hay surrounded him as he entered the stable. He strode to a middle stall, where his destrier put its head over the door and nuzzled him. Once Tristan was satisfied all was in order, he started back to the keep, but movement on the battlement caught his attention.

Illuminated by torchlight, a woman strolled the parapet: *Honoria*. She'd loosened her hair and it flowed behind her on the wind. How captivating she was, and yet, she also seemed unbearably lonely.

A heavy ache formed in his chest, for he was responsible for upsetting her.

He must go to her. His honor demanded it.

Chapter Seven

H onoria fingered windblown hair back from her face as she walked the battlement with Willow. The closest wall torch had gone out, but more burned farther down, where guards kept watch on the bailey below and the lands surrounding the castle.

The wind stung her eyes, but she didn't bother to pull up her cloak's hood. There was a wildness to the frosty night air that she loved; in the morning, the ground would glitter as if thousands of stars had fallen from the heavens.

She reached down and patted Willow, remembering how the dog had enjoyed walks with Honoria's sire. Her father had savored the crispness of icy mornings. Indeed, he'd cherished the holiday season for the way it brought family and friends together in good cheer and love.

Father, how I wish you could be with us this Christmas.

Instead, she had to deal with Tristan.

In hindsight, she wished she'd spoken differently in the hall tonight, acted differently, but she could do naught about that now.

The muffled *thud* of a door closing made her glance over her shoulder into the darkness. Willow halted and looked back, too. A guard had likely arrived to relight the torch, which meant an end to her solitude.

A man emerged from the blackness. "Honoria."

A silent groan welled inside her. "Tristan." He wasn't

wearing a cloak or gloves, which meant he'd left the hall quickly. Had he been searching for her? Worry flared as she asked, "Is all well inside?"

"I expect so."

"What do you mean? Has something happened to Mother?"

"I have not seen her since she went to her chamber. As far as I know, she is fine." He halted a few paces away. "I answered as I did because I left Cornelia and Radley together with the kissing bough. I am sure you can guess what is happening between them."

Honoria could indeed imagine. However, her brother adored Cornelia, even though the younger woman seemed oblivious to his interest. Radley wouldn't mind if she used the kissing bough on him.

"I did not intend to leave them alone for long," Tristan added, "but when I saw you up here, I thought I should come and check you are all right."

"Of course I am all right."

He studied her intently, causing a tightness to form in the pit of her stomach. "You were not all right when you quit the hall."

It seemed he, too, had been pondering what had taken place between them.

He moved nearer, close enough now to reach out and touch if she so wished. "For my idiocy tonight, I am sorry."

His apology sounded genuine this time, not akin to a command as it had done earlier. "Thank you." She couldn't allow him to bear all of the blame, though. "I am sorry, too."

His brows rose, a silent request for explanation.

She turned and set her gloved hand on the rough, mortared stone of the nearest merlon. "I realize now, after considering what happened, that I...reacted rather harshly. I regret I was intolerant. I suddenly found myself overwhelmed by my concern for the book." Her voice softened. "I was also very much missing my father."

Tristan set his hand on her shoulder. "I understand."

Honoria expected protective Willow to object to him touching her. But, the hound didn't bark or growl, merely walked over to her side and sat down.

Tristan's touch was unwavering, sure, and comforting. She savored the companionable silence, a bond forged by loss, and remembered Radley telling her that Tristan's mother had died when he was young.

Looking back at him, Honoria said, "I am not usually such an overly emotional or witless damsel."

He smiled. "You are far from overly emotional or witless. In my opinion, in the hall, you were a warrior queen, fighting for what rightfully belonged to her. I mean, you."

A blush threatened. "Please, cease."

"Do you not like thinking of yourself as a warrior queen?"

"I am hardly brave. I am not trained for battle, nor do I have royal blood running in my veins."

"Even so, I will always remember you in such a way. Regal, determined, and unforgettable…like Guinevere."

Oh, mercy. No one had ever compared her to King Arthur's wife. 'Twas a glorious compliment, but one that reminded her again of her sire and the book. She ached to remember how her father had brought those wondrous legends to life for her.

Tristan's fingers gently squeezed her shoulder. "You have gone quiet."

"I was…thinking."

"About?"

The emotions tangled up inside her intensified. How did she put into words what she was feeling? How did she say that while she appreciated his touch, it somehow made her turmoil even more complicated?

When she didn't immediately answer, his hand fell away, and he moved in beside her to gaze down into the bailey lit by torches.

The wind sighed, bringing the tang of torch smoke to Honoria, along with the faintest hint of Tristan's scent: leather and soap. The enticing smell made her long to lean in against him, close her eyes, and inhale deeply, but 'twas hardly ladylike behavior.

"Tell me your thoughts," he coaxed.

She could refuse, but she didn't want to. They'd forged a bond of trust. "I am thinking…that your kindness has made me feel even more foolish about earlier."

"We have all said and done things we later regretted."

"Have you?" she asked.

"Oh, aye."

"What happened, if you do not mind my asking?"

Tristan's visage had hardened with reticence; she'd clearly stirred up difficult emotions for him. Yet, he reached to his neck and drew out a thin cord from beneath his garments. Fastened to the cord was a small leather pouch.

He opened the bag and tipped the contents into his hand: a lock of hair, wrapped around with fine gold thread.

"A lady's hair?" she asked.

"Indeed, a lady's hair."

Odelia's tresses lay in Tristan's palm like a dangerous temptation. He closed his fingers around the token he'd kept close to his heart. He'd meant to destroy it, but then had decided to keep it as a reminder of his folly—and his vow to focus on duty, not love.

Beside him, Honoria remained silent. She was

obviously doing her best to be patient, even though she longed to know more.

He slowly opened his fingers again. When Odelia had cut the lock and placed it in his palm, a romantic gesture that had resonated with his sense of chivalry, he'd pledged his devotion to her. He'd never imagined she'd forsake him.

"Do you love her?" Honoria finally asked.

"Odelia betrayed me months ago."

"Oh, I did not realize."

"While I do not believe I loved her, I did care about her." He brushed his thumb over the silken parcel. "I thought she cared for me, but I was mistaken."

"I am sorry."

How he loathed talking about Odelia; but, he wanted Honoria to know the truth. For some reason he couldn't quite understand, he felt compelled to tell her all. "She is the daughter of an earl, and our sires are allies. When I courted her, my father was thrilled and encouraged me to wed her." Tristan laughed roughly. "My sire and I are often at odds, but when I told him I planned to marry her, I became a favored son. The union, you see, would have brought my family great renown."

"Oh, Tristan."

"She had agreed to marry me, and, as was proper, I was going to ask her father for her hand in marriage. The night before I was to speak with her sire, I found her…in another man's arms." His hand closed around the thread-wrapped hair again, while he fought fury and disappointment.

Honoria touched his arm. Her fingers pressed, offering reassurance.

He was suddenly short of breath. The air in his lungs became frozen, suspended in a tantalizing moment of possibility.

'Twas as if he'd been caught up in an enchantment.

His thoughts reeled, rekindling what he knew of the legend of Tristan and Iseult. Was this how Tristan had felt after he'd drunk the love potion?

Ah, God, but he was just so *aware* of Honoria. Sensation raced through his body: intense cognizance of her nearness; of her gaze upon him; of the floral fragrance that surrounded her.

He fought the pleasure elicited by her touch, tried to break free of the spell cast upon him.

Never again would he fall in love.

He hardened his heart to the longing to know her in all ways.

Never.

"What did your father say, when you told him of her betrayal?" Honoria asked.

The torment inside Tristan twisted like the blade of a knife. "He told me I was a fool to have ended the relationship."

"*Really?*"

"Aye. He told me I should have wed her anyway, because of all that I—and my family—would have gained."

Her fingers pressed again.

He shuddered, fighting his yearning for her.

Never....

With effort, he broke from her touch, more abruptly than he'd intended. The craving for her diminished, but 'twas still there, smoldering like an ember that could be stirred up in an instant. "My father and I have not spoken since," he added gruffly. "If there are matters he and I need to discuss, I send missives through one of my siblings."

Honoria shook her head and stared out into the darkness. "I thought all fathers were like mine; that all sires supported their children."

"In his own way, I guess my father did. He saw an opportunity for me to advance my career, increase our family's holdings—"

"At the cost of your happiness."

Tristan managed a careless shrug. "It does not matter now."

"It *does* matter. Odelia forsook you. Your sire hurt you as well."

"I will persevere."

Her eyes narrowed, and again, he saw the queen that he'd witnessed in the hall. "You are right to want a marriage founded on true love. To have children born of that love."

Damnation, but he wished she wasn't so magnificent. His gaze fell to her mouth; perfectly formed, lush lips. Suddenly, he wanted her to touch him again. Even stronger was the urge to lose himself in her kiss.

He blinked hard. What in hellfire was he thinking? He must be under that enchantment again.

"Since you are familiar with the ancient tales," Honoria was saying, "you will know they are not just love stories. They also honor knights who undertook perilous quests. Those men endured great hardships, but became heroes because of the challenges they faced."

Was she going to compare his plight to what the legendary knights had endured? How flattering.

"Mayhap what you went through recently was destined to make you stronger."

"It sure as hell will not destroy me," he said.

"I hope not."

Her hushed voice was akin to a caress; a lover's hand trailing over his naked skin. A tremor rippled through him, chased by desire. A sinful part of his conscience told him to pursue the invitation in her voice and eyes, to bury his hand into her hair, tilt up her chin, and kiss her full on the lips—a kiss to rival any she'd read about in her books.

As he stared down at her in the darkness, her mouth slightly parted, her eyes questioning, he sensed she wouldn't refuse him. He was skilled enough at kissing that he'd ensure she enjoyed it.

"Tristan?" she whispered, as if she didn't understand the struggle within him, or within herself.

God's bones, he wanted so very much to kiss her. Yet, he'd made a vow to himself. He must keep it.

Moreover, if one of the guards on the battlement opposite saw him kiss Honoria, he could find himself committed to her; the same dilemma he'd faced with Cornelia in the hall.

"I fear I have left Radley alone too long already," he said as the wind stirred his hair and garments. Somehow, he hadn't realized 'twas so bloody cold outside until now. "I should return to the hall."

She must have seen him shiver, for she asked, "Would you like to borrow my cloak?"

He laughed at the reminder of his offer in the orchard. "We can both go inside and see Radley."

"Nay, I will return to my chamber."

"Return to your tomes, you mean."

Tension defined her posture now. He hadn't meant to hurt her, but she must know that for a woman as young, beautiful, and intelligent as she was, there was far more to life than old tales.

He returned the lock of hair to its leather pouch and tucked it under his shirt. "With your knowledge of the old stories, you will recall that the heroines had to endure difficult trials too."

Surprise and wariness registered in her expression. "I am aware—"

"Good. Then I trust you will not allow your hardships to destroy you. You are destined for far greater things."

Honoria stared at him, her mouth agape.

He longed to say more, but he'd already said more

than was wise. He bowed and strode away, leaving her to finish her walk.

Sitting up in bed with the book of tales, Honoria sighed and slumped back against her pillows. For some annoying reason, she couldn't stop thinking about her conversation with Tristan. His words echoed over and over: *Do not allow your hardships to destroy you.*

What gave him the right to comment on her situation? 'Twas clear he didn't understand at all. She wasn't being destroyed by her grief; she was mourning her beloved father, as a daughter should.

Wasn't she?

Beside her on the bed, Willow pawed her hip. Honoria scratched the dog's chin. "You understand, do you not, Willow?"

The hound's shaggy tail thumped on the coverlet, and she licked Honoria's hand.

"Tristan was most bold to say what he did." He'd been rather bold in other matters, too. His gaze had held a kind of hunger, one that had made her grow warm with a delicious heat. What, exactly, did it mean when a lord looked upon a lady in that way?

After he'd left her on the parapet, she'd gone straight to her chamber. She'd disrobed by the hearth, pulled on her chemise, and climbed into bed, hoping to ease her restlessness by reading. Usually, that worked. Tonight, it had not.

She turned the next few pages, wishing there was more detail on what happened right before a knight and a damsel kissed. How did the lady feel when she sensed the kiss was about to happen? Did she experience that delicious heat?

Mayhap she could ask Radley. He'd been kissing women since he was twelve. Yet, such questions would reveal to him just now ignorant she really was, and she couldn't bear such humiliation.

Setting the tome aside, Honoria blew out the bedside candles and lay back. Firelight threw shifting shadows across the ceiling.

Do not allow your hardships to destroy you.

She scowled. On the morrow, she'd show Tristan she wasn't allowing life to pass her by.

She *was* a lady who overcame obstacles and became stronger for them.

Chapter Eight

"Lord de Bretagne has just ridden into the bailey, milady."

"Thank you." With a nod to the man-at-arms, who quit the hall, Lady Whitford set down the gold silk bliaut she'd been mending by the fire; the one she intended to wear on Christmas Day.

Honoria had been making centerpieces of beeswax candles, pine cones, and evergreens. She hurried to her parent's side, sliding her arm through her mother's as she stood.

"Guillaume always enjoys the boar hunt," Lady Whitford said. "He will be eager to ride to the forest as soon as possible."

Honoria smiled. "There *are* only two days left before Christmas." Radley had vowed to follow the same customs as their sire when he'd become lord, and that included serving the boar's head on a silver platter on Christmas Day.

Her mother winked as they headed for the forebuilding stairs. "The feast just wouldn't be same without the boar, would it?"

Honoria murmured her agreement while trying not to grimace. She'd never liked the taste of roasted boar, and didn't particularly enjoy seeing the wild pig's head displayed with an apple in its mouth, but she understood her brother's wish to preserve their family's traditions.

When Honoria and her mother walked out into the chilly but sun-drenched bailey, Guillaume was standing beside his destrier and talking with Radley. When the older lord saw them, he waved and crossed to them, his hair white in the sunshine.

"Valerie, my love."

Guillaume embraced Lady Whitford and kissed her on the lips. Honoria knew without doubt that he adored her mother. That soul-deep love lauded in the old tales was real and powerful: The kind of love Tristan wanted and that Honoria wanted too, some day.

After one more kiss, Guillaume drew back, holding her ladyship at arm's length.

"You are well, Honoria?" he asked.

"I am."

"She finished decorating the hall this morning," said Lady Whitford. "It looks splendid. So does the kissing bough she and Cornelia made together."

"Where is my daughter?" Guillaume asked.

"She complained of a headache this morning," Honoria said. "She decided to stay abed and rest."

"Ah. Well, please give her my regards. I will see her after the hunt."

The *clip-clop* of horses' hooves drew Honoria's gaze to the stable. Tristan, Sydney, and several other men-at-arms had emerged, leading their mounts. Tristan made an impressive figure in his forest-green woolen cloak and knee-high boots. Catching her gaze, he nodded to her before he was lost to her view among the other riders and horses.

Memories of last night on the battlement rushed into her mind. Had Tristan wanted to kiss her? Or had she imagined his interest, her romantic soul interpreting the shadows so that she discerned hunger when in truth he didn't care for her in that way at all?

Honoria truly did want to know how it felt to be

kissed by a man, and before she turned twenty. Surely that proved she wasn't letting life pass her by? She suddenly realized she could *show* Tristan how much she was taking initiative in her own life *and* find out how he felt about her.

She could kiss him. On the mouth.

If no one witnessed the intimacy, Tristan wouldn't be honor-bound to make a lasting commitment to her, and Cornelia wouldn't get upset.

And finally, *finally*, Honoria would know what a real kiss was like.

Excitement swirled up inside her, even as her brother asked, "Will you be ready to depart soon, Guillaume?"

The older lord tucked stray hair behind Lady Whitford's ear. "I am ready now."

"Be careful, Radley," her ladyship pleaded. "Boars are unpredictable creatures. Remember how your father was injured during a hunt? I do not want anyone hurt this year."

"Mother, do not fret," Radley said. "All will be well."

Tristan crept through the forest shadows, his dagger poised to strike. The other hunters, many of them wielding boar spears, moved from tree to tree a short distance to Tristan's left, drawing nearer to their prey that had already found them. Startled while foraging, the male boar had attacked and narrowly missed gouging Guillaume with its curved tusks.

Through the undergrowth ahead, Tristan sighted the beast near a fallen log, its sides heaving, an arrow buried in its left flank. Radley signaled a halt.

His body taut with anticipation, Tristan crouched behind a straggly bush. Soon, the woods would erupt in the chaos that ensued before the animal was cornered and killed.

"Now!" Radley yelled.

Crashing footfalls sounded. Shouts echoed.

Tristan raced out from behind the bush.

The squinty-eyed beast barreled toward them. Guillaume fired; another arrow pierced the boar's hide. The animal recoiled and squealed again in pain and fury. Spying Tristan, it lowered its head to attack.

"Beware," Radley yelled.

Tristan tightened his grip on his dagger. He counted heartbeats as he waited for just the right moment....

He lunged, bringing his knife down.

At the same instant, a spear plowed into the animal's neck. It flailed its head, staggered to the right, spattering blood.

"Tristan!" Radley cried.

Mid-swing, Tristan turned and tried to adjust the fall of his knife. The musky stink of the animal assaulted his senses, right before the boar's tusks ripped into his right thigh.

"Try to eat some of this bread and cheese." Honoria handed Cornelia the wooden tray she'd brought, laden with fare and a mug of wine. The younger woman did look a bit wan sitting in bed against the whiteness of her mounded pillows; some food inside her might help—and encourage her to divulge what was really bothering her. She'd seemed perfectly hale earlier last night in the hall, so whatever ailed her must have happened after Honoria had left.

Had Cornelia been unsuccessful in winning a kiss from Tristan using the kissing bough? 'Twas the most likely reason for her sulking.

"Come on," Honoria coaxed, for the younger woman had not yet tried the food. "The bread is soft and flavorful today."

Willow licked her lips. She sat very obediently beside Honoria, obviously hoping perfect behavior would win her a treat from the tray.

"Fine, I will eat. Mayhap then, you will stop pestering me."

As a scowling Cornelia picked up some cheese, a faint sound carried in through the open window: the peal of a hunting horn. Honoria had opened the shutters earlier to let in some fresh air.

Cornelia huddled deeper into her blankets. "For God's sake, shut—"

"Hush." Honoria hurried to the window and strained to hear. If Radley was blasting the horn, that meant—

"*Hush*? 'Tis my chamber. If I feel cold—"

"Please. *Listen*."

Grumbling, Cornelia fell silent.

The blast of a horn carried once more, louder this time.

"Someone is hurt," the younger woman whispered.

"Aye."

Cornelia set aside the tray, rose, and crossed to stand with Honoria at the window. "Are the riders far from the castle? Can you tell who has been injured?"

A metallic creak sounded as the portcullis rose. Honoria leaned into the window embrasure. "I cannot see or hear from here. We will need to go to the bailey."

"Help me dress. I must know Father is all right."

Honoria fetched a clean chemise and helped Cornelia don the undergarment and a gown. With Willow leading the way, they went to the bailey to meet the arriving hunting party. A dead boar, its tongue lolling and arrows sticking out of its hide, was tied to a man-at-arms' horse.

Honoria breathed a silent prayer of thanks that her brother was unharmed. Guillaume, riding a short distance behind with Sydney, also seemed all right. Who, then—?

"Get water on to boil," Radley called to a servant as he reined in his destrier. "Summon the healer."

"Milord, the healer left this morn," one of the stable hands said. "She went to visit her sister."

"Damnation, I remember now."

"Tristan!" Cornelia shrieked.

Honoria choked down a shocked cry. His ashen face was beaded with sweat, and when he urged his mount toward a water trough, she saw blood on the right side of his cloak.

"Oh, Tristan." Cornelia hurried to him.

"What happened?" Honoria asked.

"He was cut by the boar's tusks before it fell," Radley said grimly.

Her stomach lurched, as if she was braving across a wind-churned lake on a tiny raft. "How bad is the wound?"

"Not so deep."

"Are you certain?"

"I saw the injury when he washed it by the stream. While it may not be life-threatening, I am sure 'tis painful."

His arm slung over Sydney's shoulders, Tristan limped toward them, Cornelia at his side. Tristan smiled, although the mirth was clearly forced. "Do not worry. I will live."

"You look ready to collapse." Concern rendered Honoria's tone sharper than she'd intended.

A muscle ticked in Tristan's cheek, and he straightened slightly. "I will not collapse, I promise you."

Annoyance hummed in her veins. He didn't want to admit to his discomfort in front of the other men. Was he afraid of appearing weak, or less of a knight, because he'd been hurt?

He might have rinsed his wound, but it had already gone a while without being properly cleaned; corruption could easily set in. She must get him inside so she could examine it.

"With our healer away," Radley said, "we will need to get him to the surgeon in the next town."

"I will treat him," Honoria said.

Tristan's brows rose, as if he couldn't quite believe he'd heard correctly.

"Sis, you are a lady. Gently-bred noblewomen do not—"

"Do not be silly. I helped the healer care for Father. Remember?"

"So you did," her brother conceded.

"If the healer's ointments do not work quickly enough, there is also a remedy in the book I bought at the market."

Cornelia rolled her eyes. "You and your books."

The disquiet inside Honoria sharpened; she *had* to make the others understand. "The wound has already gone too long without care. 'Tis surely better than I treat it now, rather than make Tristan get back on his horse and travel to the town that is some distance from here."

"That does make sense," Tristan agreed.

Guillaume, who had joined them, frowned. "He needs stitches. That man-at-arms who has treated battle wounds might be better—"

Honoria shook her head. "I can do stitches."

"I guess the final decision is really Tristan's," Radley said. "What do you say, Tris?"

The faintest doubt still lingered in Tristan's expression, but he nodded to Honoria.

Relief washed through her. Summoning one of the maidservants, she said, "Bring the boiled water to the chamber where Lord de Champagne is staying, along with wine, cloths, and towels."

The servant curtsied and hurried away.

Honoria met her brother's gaze. "You and Sydney must carry Tristan to his bed."

Tristan scowled. "I can walk."

"You will be carried. Walking might aggravate your injury. Also, Mother will not want blood on the floors."

Tristan's mouth snapped shut.

"Once Tristan is in his room, help him remove his garments," Honoria said. "'Twill be easier for me to treat him. Now, get him inside, before he falls to the dirt. Cornelia, you are with me."

As the ladies and Willow walked toward the keep, Tristan exhaled a harsh breath and lowered his shoulders. Maintaining a proud façade in front of Honoria had taken effort with his thigh throbbing and his gut churning with the pain. He'd be glad to get away from the noisy bailey and to rest a while.

He winced as Radley instructed him to stand without help. Hell, he'd planned to drink, dance, and make merry all through Christmas. Mayhap if he was careful now, he'd have recovered enough to enjoy at least some of the celebrating.

"All right, Tris. Sit," Radley said.

He and the steward had crossed their arms to form a makeshift seat. Tristan sat, and as if he were some ancient king who didn't deign to get dirt on his boots, they carried him into the keep and up to his chamber.

When they entered his room, where a freshly stoked fire burned, disquiet trailed through him, for he realized he hadn't really thought through Honoria tending to his wound. She wanted him undressed. That meant her bare hands would be moving on his *bare* flesh: a circumstance that could make him face a whole other kind of physical weakness. He did have feelings for her, as his yearning to kiss her last night proved.

Regardless of his desire, he must ignore even the slightest flicker of interest in her. Honoria had offered to treat him, not pleasure him. He would keep a firm hold on his thoughts and cravings. While she tended him, he'd mentally block out all awareness of her scent, her nearness, above all the touch of her slender hands gliding—

"Are you all right?" Radley asked, as they lowered him onto the chair by the bed.

"I will feel better after a few goblets of wine."

"I will bring you some of my best." Radley ordered Sydney to take away the bed's silk coverlet so it wouldn't get soiled with blood. Then, after dismissing the steward, he pushed the linen sheets and woolen blanket down to the end of the straw-stuffed mattress.

"Honoria wanted you to remove your clothes," Radley said.

As if he needed a reminder. Tristan's loins heated at the thought of her seeing him almost naked; he forced the ridiculous anticipation into submission.

"Can you manage by yourself, or do you want my help?"

Just thinking about stripping off his hose—the jostling of his lower body, the tugging on his hurting limb— made Tristan's head reel. "You will need to assist me. I want to be abed when Honoria arrives."

"All right." Radley shut the chamber door and returned to the bedside. "I must ask a favor of you, though."

"What is that?"

"When Honoria is with you, keep the door open. 'Tis wisest for both of you. I do not want her maidenly reputation to be in question."

"Agreed." Tristan stood and then sat on the edge of the mattress; the bed ropes creaked at his weight.

Radley crouched and carefully pulled off Tristan's left boot. "Truth be told, if I thought there was even the slightest chance of anything scandalous happening, I would not let her treat you. I know you are an honorable man, Tris."

Not according to his father, he wasn't. If his sire was to be believed, Tristan had ruined his life and sullied the honor of his entire family—misdeeds that could never be forgiven.

Radley set aside the boot. When he reached for the right one, Tristan braced himself for an onslaught of pain.

Cornelia paced Honoria's chamber, her headache clearly forgotten. Willow lay near the bed, keeping watch.

"Poor Tristan," the younger woman said. "What a terrible thing to have happened to him."

Only half-listening, Honoria changed into an older gown; it wouldn't matter if it got stained with blood and herbs.

"Tristan *has* to be better for Christmas."

"Radley said the wound is not deep." Honoria smoothed her bodice. "If 'tis so, there is no reason why Tristan cannot enjoy most of the festivities."

Cornelia sighed as though 'twas exactly what she'd hoped to hear. "Good, because Christmas is *not* going to come and go without him kissing me, and not just once under the kissing bough."

Honoria stilled in the midst of rolling up her sleeves. The younger woman was peering into a mirror of polished steel and pinching her cheeks, as she would before meeting a suitor. "Tristan is hurt," Honoria said, fighting for patience, "and all you can think about is kissing him?"

Cornelia banged down the mirror. "Tristan *is* going to be my betrothed, as I told you before."

A surge of jealousy and anguish welled up inside Honoria. Uncertain how deal with such strong emotions, she went to the table where she'd set out her small wooden box containing bone needles and thread. Sucking in a calming breath, she tried to focus on gathering what she needed to tend to Tristan's injury.

"While his wound is unfortunate, I have come to realize what I must do," Cornelia said. "I will sit at his bedside to prove how much I care for him. I will help him sip broth, wipe sweat from his brow, wash his face, comb the tangles from his hair—"

Honoria fought the urge to scream.

"He will see that I am a lady with a tender nature, who will be the perfect mother for his children." Cornelia twirled around, her gown floating at her ankles. "He will not be able to resist me."

"I am sure he will appreciate your visits while he recuperates. In the meanwhile," Honoria said, "I was hoping you could fetch some things for me?"

"Aye, I am happy to help."

"I need the pot of yellow salve the healer keeps in her workshop."

"I will get it for you. What else?"

Honoria had to clean the wound before she applied the salve, and that would go more quickly without Cornelia hovering over Tristan and possibly getting in the way. "I may also need to use a poultice." She fetched her late sire's herbal and jotted the list of ingredients on a spare piece of parchment. "Bring the items to Tristan's room when you have gathered them."

"I shall." Clutching the list, the younger woman quit

the chamber.

Honoria picked up her box. Jealousy and anguish still churned inside her, but she mustn't dwell on those fickle emotions. While earlier she'd thought about kissing Tristan, that desire seemed silly and selfish now. He was hurt. She'd taken responsibility for his care, and now she must do all she could to ensure that he recovered.

His wellbeing took priority over a kiss.

The wolfhound nuzzled her leg and stared up at her with baleful eyes.

"Aye, Willow. I must get to work."

Chapter Nine

Honoria approached Tristan's room. Voices carried into the corridor from the open doorway: her brother's and Tristan's. The unmistakable timbre of Tristan's voice sent a hot-cold shiver racing through her.

Radley, sitting in the chair by the bed, was telling of an amusing mistake he'd made while keeping the castle accounts. Tristan lay on his back on the mattress, his right arm folded across his stomach and his left one running alongside his body. A rolled towel lay against his blood-covered thigh. Another towel hid his male parts, while blankets covered him from the upper leg down.

Her brother noticed her first. "Honoria."

Tristan met her gaze. The mattress rustled as he attempted to sit up; no doubt he meant to greet her properly, despite his injury, but the towel over his loins would fall away—

"Please, be still," she said.

He fell back against the pillows.

Ignoring the wild fluttering of her pulse, she instructed Willow to stay in the passageway and entered the room.

While she walked to the table, she cast a quick glance over Tristan. Mother Mary, but he was a magnificent sight, all bronzed and muscled against the cream-colored bed linens. His broad chest, an impressive display of honed muscles and gleaming skin, led down to his flat stomach and the trail of dark hairs disappearing under the towel.

How unconscionable that part of her was curious about the bulge beneath the cloth. She'd seen naked men before, washing in the bailey after weapons practice, so she knew what masculine parts looked like, but still....

She forced her wayward mind to focus. Thankfully, the servants had already delivered the items she'd requested. Buckets of steaming water waited near the bed, and towels, rags, and bowls had been left on the table, along with a large jug of wine. She set down the box and washed her hands with water and wine, feeling Tristan's gaze traveling over her back as she did so.

She faced the bed.

"Do you need my help, Sis?"

"Nay, I can manage."

Tristan's eyes were closed now. He must be in discomfort.

Radley stood. "I have some matters to attend, but will check in on Tristan later."

"Would you mind taking Willow with you? I do not want her coming in here while I am working on the wound."

"Of course." Radley left, leaving the chamber door open. He called the wolfhound to him and strode away.

Honoria carried a bowl of water to the right side of the bed and set it down on the planks. When she knelt beside Tristan, she caught the masculine scent of him; earthy and enticing. Just as she remembered from last night.

Heat spread across her skin; he'd turned his head on the pillow and was watching her. Unable to deny the impulse, she met his piercing stare.

She couldn't look away. As though she'd been entranced, she was suddenly, acutely, aware of the intense quietude, broken only by the crackling of the fire; his measured breathing; the softness of the linen bedding beneath her hand. Her fingers tightened on the rag she held.

"You do not have to tend me, if you really do not want to," he said.

"Oh, cease." She wasn't going to retreat now. Like the legendary heroines she admired, she must do what needed to be done.

"*Cease?*" Wry amusement shone in Tristan's eyes. "Do you speak to all of your patients in that manner?"

"Only the challenging ones."

"I did not realize I was being difficult. I thought I was being most obedient, undressing and getting into bed as you had asked."

Put that way, her instructions sounded scandalous. A wanton tremor ran through her, and to distract herself, she dropped the rag into the water.

"If I am too much of a challenge—"

"You are not." She wrung out the cloth. "Trust me, you are better off with me than the man-at-arms Guillaume recommended."

"Why is that?"

"The man-at-arms does not see well these days. I would hate for him to sew your arm to your thigh."

As she'd hoped, she caught a hint of a smile on Tristan's lips.

She studied the wound. "I am going to begin. I will do my best not to hurt you."

"I know you will."

The genuine understanding in his voice brought a lump to her throat. She gently washed away the dried blood. The boar's tusks had gouged furrows into his skin, and the area around the wound was turning purple with nasty bruising, but he'd been lucky; the damage could have been much worse. However, a few stitches would help the wound heal faster.

After thoroughly rinsing the injury with water, she fetched the wine. Tristan had drawn sharp breaths while she'd worked, but otherwise, had remained still, his eyes shut.

A lock of dark, shiny hair had fallen over his cheek, and as she knelt again, she yearned to sweep it back off his face. What would the skin of his cheek feel like beneath her fingertips? Was his hair soft, like hers, or coarse, like her brother's?

She mentally dismissed the foolish longing. She might startle him with that unexpected touch and thereby increase his pain, or—heaven forbid—cause him to dislodge the towel.

The piquant smell of wine wafted as she used it to rinse the wound. He flinched, but didn't cry out. She fetched the bone needle and some thread. Returning to the bedside, she said, "I am going to do a few stitches now."

"Fine." His voice was drowsy, as if she'd lured him from the edge of sleep.

Her hand trembled a little—she'd stitched Willow's wounds but never a knight's before—while she carefully sewed the edges of torn flesh closed.

Pleased with the way the stitches had turned out, she sat back on her heels. Tristan lay motionless. Silent.

Had he suffered so much pain, he'd fainted?

She rose up on her knees and leaned sideways on the bed to study his face. His thick lashes lay against his skin. His lips, as full and sensual as she imagined the most romantic knights' to be, were slightly pursed.

"Tristan?" she whispered.

"Mmm?" he said softly, his eyes remaining shut.

Was that an admission of pain, or mere acknowledgement that she'd spoken to him?

"Are you well?"

His throat moved with a swallow, but he didn't reply.

Surely, if he was all right, he'd have opened his eyes

and answered her.

Concern welled up inside her, overruling the voice of reason that cautioned her to move back. She eased closer still, lured by his scent and the warmth of his body. A *knight's* body.

His mouth was a mere breath away. She could steal a kiss and finally know what it felt like to kiss a man.

She shouldn't.

Yet, she wanted to. *So* very much.

Never before had she felt such urgency—as if her very soul, her very life, depended upon it. How was it possible to crave so intensely? 'Twas as if she'd been caught up in some kind of magic, and the only way to break the spell was to press her lips to Tristan's.

Kiss him, her conscience whispered. *Hurry, for it might be your only chance.*

She would not let life pass her by.

Before she could stifle the impulse, she pressed her mouth to his.

His eyes closed, Tristan tried to focus on something other than Honoria. He tallied how many goblets of wine he'd downed last night; how many days were left until he was traveling to London; hell, *anything* to keep from thinking about the beautiful woman so close by.

Her floral scent teased him every time he inhaled. The whispering of her gown reminded him of sheets tangling as lovers kissed, caressed, and with impassioned gasps, surrendered fully to their carnal desires. And the gentleness of her fingers on his skin....

He must be mad, or under that enchantment he'd experienced last night. Even while he was enduring pain, he experienced a stirring of lust. A damned awkward stirring, when all he had to conceal his swelling interest was a towel.

Ah, God, he'd vowed to be honorable, but his body was betraying him.

Mayhap she wouldn't notice?

And then, he felt the softness of her lips upon his.

His eyes flew open. Her face was near his, her eyes still shut, as though she was savoring the sensations elicited by the kiss. She was exquisite, her skin dewy, her lips as red as wild strawberries.

Had he been her first kiss? The throbbing in his groin intensified.

Slowly, her eyes opened.

She blinked, clearly startled to see him staring at her. Her cheeks reddened, and she abruptly drew back.

"Honoria—"

"I…I am sorry. I—"

"Please. Do not fret."

"I should not have kissed you." Fumbling with the rag, she pushed up from the bedside.

"Wait. Why did you kiss me?"

She stilled and then sank back to her knees. Her mortified gaze met his and then darted away again. "I thought…. I was worried you had fainted because of the pain."

Disappointment coursed through him. "You didn't kiss me, then, because you wanted to."

"Oh, I did want to." She sighed. "You will think me foolish if I tell you the truth."

"Not at all. I really would like to know."

She bit down on her lower lip; he longed to rise up on his elbow, sink his hand into her hair, and kiss her, right there where she'd bitten. "I…wanted to be like the damsels in the old tales. I longed to know what it was like to kiss a knight." She swallowed hard. "Not just any knight, but…you."

He fought a proud smile. "I see."

"I was wrong to have done so. You trusted me to treat your wound, and…."

"Honoria."

"I acted on an impulse I should have ignored, as I have ignored it ever since you arrived."

Astonishment ripped through him. "You have wanted to kiss me since we first met?"

Her blush intensified, making her cheekbones even more pronounced. She nodded. "My yearning for you…. I cannot explain it, but I cannot deny it, either."

She was experiencing the same intense feelings for him as he was for her?

"I should not have told you," she whispered.

"I am glad you did."

"You are?"

He nodded against the pillow. "'Twas a very nice kiss." If she glanced at his lower body, she'd see just how enticing it had been. He stifled his annoying conscience reminding him of his promise to be honorable and said: "If you like, we can kiss again. A bit longer this time, so you can fully experience what 'tis like."

With a soft *plop*, the rag landed in the bowl of water. She seemed both eager and uncertain.

"You will have first-hand knowledge, then, to draw upon when reading the tales." He couldn't let her go now; he was starving for her kiss, even more than he'd been last night.

"What if someone sees us?" She sounded breathless, as if she'd just run up a long flight of stairs. "Cornelia will be bringing some items—"

"Then we must be quick."

His conscience cried out again; 'twas overruled by his hunger. He carefully lifted his right arm, curved it around her upper body, and urged her toward him. He half-expected her to resist, but she moved easily, allowing him to slide his hand up her back and into her plaited hair. How silky her tresses felt against his fingers.

She leaned down, her essence flooding his senses, and kissed him.

The touch of her lips sent heat racing through him. As her mouth pressed to his in the most innocent of kisses, he moved his lips beneath hers, encouraging her to explore him. If she was willing, he'd teach her all the nuances of kissing.

She exhaled against his mouth, and her lips followed his, matching his kisses, becoming caught up in the sensual exploration.

Ah, God, but he'd never been this aroused from kissing a woman.

Desire became a demanding, fiery need within him. As they kissed, he slid his tongue between her lips to taste her. She shuddered and then slipped her tongue into his mouth, and he groaned at the pleasure. His fingers tightened in her hair. He wanted her, far more than he dared admit.

He should stop kissing her. He should stop touching her—

Her breath fanned his damp lips, and she caught his bottom lip with her teeth. She suckled, nipped, and kissed as if she couldn't contain her rising passion any longer, and with such incredible skill, he groaned again. Helpless to resist, he opened his mouth to her, and their tongues clashed, slick heat to slick heat.

She moaned in awe.

He couldn't fight his desire any longer. He kissed her hard, fast, their breaths mingling.

Over their muffled gasps, he caught a faint sound.

Someone was drawing near.

Stop, his conscience cried. *Now!*

The warning tore into the haze of need fogging his mind. Before he could wrest his mouth away, Cornelia cried: "Honoria! How could you?"

Chapter Ten

Honoria froze. Beneath her, Tristan stilled too, his mouth still touching hers.

She pulled away from him, her lips tingling. She'd been soaring on the most incredible pleasure; it had shattered the instant she'd realized they weren't alone.

Cornelia stood at the end of the bed, holding a tray with the salve and poultice ingredients Honoria had requested. The younger woman looked angry enough to drop the lot on the floor.

"Honoria," Cornelia shrilled.

Shame taunted her as she pushed to standing. "Please, I was—"

"I know *what* you were doing. I saw."

Honoria took the tray and set it on the bed, all the while scrambling to think of a reasonable explanation for what she'd done. She didn't want to speak falsely, not to a friend. Not when kissing Tristan had been the most thrilling experience *ever*.

The bed rustled behind her. "'Twas my fault," he said. Somehow, he'd pulled the blanket up to his waist. She might have scolded him for straining his wound, but sensed he'd had a reason for adjusting the bedding—and 'twasn't that he'd been cold.

Cornelia glowered. "How is what happened your fault, Tristan?"

"I asked her for a kiss. One to help me heal faster."

Honoria shook her head. Tristan was being most gallant, but she couldn't let him accept responsibility. "Tristan is not to blame for the kiss. I am."

Anguish filled the younger woman's gaze. "Why would you do such a thing, when I told you…?" Her words died on a furious sob.

"I am sorry," Honoria said softly. "I could not help myself."

"Could not *help* yourself? He was to be *mine*."

"Wait just one moment," Tristan said firmly. "Not once did I—"

"I thought we were friends." Cornelia wiped away tears running down her cheeks. "I trusted you."

Guilt twisted up inside Honoria. "I did not mean to hurt you."

"But you did. That you would be so deceitful at *Christmas* makes it all the worse!" Wailing, the younger woman dashed from the chamber.

Honoria pressed her hand to her still-tingling mouth. How would she ever make matters right with Cornelia?

A bone-deep chill settled within her. If the younger woman told any of the castle folk about the kiss, Honoria's virtue would be in doubt. No lord would want to marry her if he believed she was ruined.

"Oh, God," she murmured.

"Oh, God, indeed."

Her traitorous heart quickened at the fetching sight Tristan made, his hair spilling like ink against the pillow, his eyes soulful. She longed to sit beside him and kiss him again, consequences be damned…but she mustn't.

She picked up the items she'd used to treat his wound and carried them to the table.

"If there is any question as to what happened between us, I am prepared to accept all of the blame."

She couldn't let him do that. She'd initiated the kiss; thus, she must take responsibility. There had to be a way to resolve the situation, if only she knew what 'twas.

"Honoria," Tristan insisted.

Determined to keep a firm hold on her desires, she returned to the bedside, picked up the salve from the tray, and lifted back the edge of the bedding to check he hadn't torn any stitches. Thankfully, he hadn't.

"If you want to go to Cornelia, I will be fine."

"I will visit her shortly." Honoria pulled the cork stopper from the pot, releasing a strong herbal scent. "I promised to care for your injury, and I will." She leaned down and dabbed salve on his damaged flesh.

He laughed roughly. "You regret kissing me."

The bluntness of his words hurt, but she wouldn't lie to protect herself. Applying more of the thick, greenish salve, she said, "I do not regret our kiss."

"Good, because I sure as hell do not."

Surprise flickered inside her, along with a poignant flare of joy. "You cannot mean that."

"I meant every word. I enjoyed kissing you. If the choice were mine, I would be kissing you again. Right now. Until you begged me to stop."

Oh, mercy. He shouldn't say such wicked things. She wanted to respond, but heard someone drawing near.

A small wine cask tucked under his arm, Radley entered the chamber. "How is—?" As his focus shifted from Tristan to her, his expression sobered. "What is going on?"

Honoria's grip tightened on the pot. "I—"

"I kissed Honoria," Tristan said. "I am clearly not as honorable as you and I expected."

"Tell me what happened," Radley demanded.

Tristan ran his hand over his face. A short while ago, Honoria had set the salve on the trestle table and left, and Radley had shut the door behind her so he and Tristan could speak in private.

"As I said, I kissed your sister."

Pacing the space between the bed and the table, Radley asked, "By accident?"

Tristan stifled a brittle laugh. They both knew 'twas not possible to kiss a noble lady, of all women, by accident. "Nay."

Radley halted, his eyes blazing. "On purpose, then."

Tristan weighed his words carefully. "I wanted to kiss her. I have done since I first met her."

"Why did you not tell me before?"

"I never imagined I would have the chance to kiss her, outside of the quick, meaningless kisses that are part of holiday revelry. I had vowed not to become involved with another woman—"

"I know! You told me." Radley's lips flattened. "After your eloquent words about being an honorable man, I trusted you completely."

"And I failed you."

Just as Tristan had failed his sire.

The pain in Tristan's thigh reminded him all too well that he was mortal and fallible. He tried to shift his position, to better see his friend, but grimaced at the discomfort. Radley must have noticed, because he moved to the bedside.

"I regret disappointing you," Tristan ground out, "but I will *not* say I wish the kiss had never happened."

Radley's gaze sharpened. "You intended to ruin my sister's reputation?"

God's blood! "Of course not."

"Then you had best explain."

"'Twas a fine kiss. One of the best I have ever had."

As though stunned by the revelation, Radley sank down into the chair. "I find myself torn between the urge to rejoice and the desire to throttle you. Tris, you kissed my little sister—"

"An exquisite young woman—"

"Who could be *ruined* because of what happened in this chamber."

True. Cornelia could be confiding in the household gossips right now. Tristan could only hope that the younger woman wouldn't be so cruel.

Resolve glowed like a hot, bright flame within him, for he might have failed others in his life, but he wouldn't allow Honoria to suffer for the pleasure they'd shared. "I promise you, all will be well."

"How?"

"I have an idea, but I will need your help."

Honoria knocked on the closed door. "Cornelia."

"Go away," the younger woman answered.

"Please, let me in."

"I said, *go away!*" Muffled sobs came from inside the room, and Honoria fought a renewed wave of guilt. Mayhap she should leave Cornelia alone for a while.

Nay. She couldn't leave her friend so distraught. She pressed down on the door handle and the panel swung inward.

Cornelia stood at the open window, her back to the door. As Honoria entered, the younger woman's posture stiffened, and she dried her eyes with a handkerchief.

"I was hoping we could talk."

"What more is there to say?" Cornelia snapped, while

staring out the window. "What I saw made the situation perfectly clear."

"I never set out to hurt you."

With a harsh sob, the younger woman whirled around. "You do not understand, do you? Why I ever thought you did…."

"Understand what?" Hating to see her friend in such torment, Honoria moved closer. "Please, tell me."

The younger woman's features etched with anguish. After a silence, she said, "I just…want someone to love me, to care for me enough to make me his wife."

The agony in Cornelia's voice was truly heart-wrenching.

"You are so clever, Honoria, and interesting, and elegant—"

Mother Mary.

"And I have this." She pointed to her blemished cheek. "When a man looks at me, he sees I am imperfect, and he does not want me."

"That is not true. You are very beautiful—"

"Do you know, I was not even supposed to be traveling the day of the accident, but Mother wanted me to accompany her?" Cornelia sniffled. "Part of me wishes I had never agreed to go, for I suggested…that we take a different route than usual, and…that is why we crashed."

Honoria longed to embrace the younger woman, but sensed Cornelia wouldn't accept such comforting from her. "What happened was *not* your fault. You could not have known the storm would make that road perilous."

Dabbing at her eyes, the younger woman said, "That day changed everything for me."

It had, and not just for her. Yet, there was no reason at all why she couldn't marry once she'd found the right man—one who would treasure her and nurture her interests and talents.

"I thought Tristan might be different, that he might see me for more than my scar," Cornelia continued, hugging herself. "I was wrong."

Honoria touched her friend's arm. "There are many other lords who might be right for you, including Radley. My brother—"

"I wanted Tristan."

"I know you did, but he does not feel the same way about you."

Cornelia shrugged off Honoria's touch. "He might have done, except *you* pursued him."

Honoria's torment gouged deeper. "I never expected to have romantic feelings for him."

"Or want to kiss him, like the damsels in the old stories?"

Cornelia's taunting words stung, but Honoria merely nodded. "Just like in the old stories."

The younger woman snorted in disgust. "Say what you will, but I do not believe you. You stole Tristan from me. I will *never* forgive you."

Chapter Eleven

December 24

Honoria opened the shutters at her chamber window to reveal a gray, overcast sky. She shivered in the frigid breeze and hoped that today, Christmas Eve, would be much better than yesterday, when Cornelia had avoided Honoria. At mealtimes, the younger woman had sat with her father at the opposite end of the table to Honoria and had left the hall as soon as the meal was finished, instead of staying to chat or embroider by the hearth.

Earlier yesterday, Radley had ridden off with several guards to settle grievances between two farmers with neighboring lands, and hadn't returned until late afternoon. Radley had assigned a man-at-arms to care for Tristan's wound, so Honoria had wrapped the gifts she'd purchased in pieces of linen and tied them with twine, and had spent the afternoon with her mother.

Tristan had rested in bed most of the day, but had kept her and her mother company by the fire in the evening. While he hadn't mentioned kissing again, and neither had Honoria, the memory of their stolen intimacy had glinted in his eyes when their gazes had met. Sitting near him had made her feel alive with a glorious awareness she'd struggled to contain.

But she had. Kissing Tristan had caused tremendous upheaval. After being awake most of last night thinking about the situation, Honoria still wasn't sure what to do about it. Mayhap a morning walk would enlighten her.

Honoria fastened her cloak and headed to the bailey. She passed under the kissing bough, hanging from the archway separating the hall from the forebuilding stairs down to the bailey, on the way. No else was coming or going at the same moment, though, so no berries were picked or kisses were stolen—although some obviously had been, likely by the servants, because there were fewer berries than before.

Outside, a line of peasants bringing their rents ran underneath the gatehouse and across the lowered drawbridge. Radley was greeting the visitors, shaking hands and ruffling children's hair, just like their late sire had done. She smiled wistfully, for in so many ways, Radley was like their father.

There seemed to be more men-at-arms on duty at the gatehouse and in the bailey, however, than usual on Christmas Eve. Surely Radley didn't expect fights or thievery among the peasants? Or was there another reason for the increase in guards?

"I think he enjoys meeting his tenants," said a male voice. She turned to see Tristan walking toward her with only the slightest limp.

"I believe he does, too. How is your wound?" 'Twas a good sign that he was dressed and didn't feel the need to stay abed.

"My thigh still hurts, but 'tis less painful than yesterday," he said. "Thanks, no doubt, to your fine stitches and that smelly but effective salve."

She laughed.

"Ah. There is the smile I was hoping to see."

Honoria sobered. Wishing she didn't ache inside, she looked back at the folk.

"Cornelia will come around, you will see." Tristan had obviously noticed the younger woman's behavior yesterday. So had Honoria's mother, but when asked, Honoria had merely said she and Cornelia had had a disagreement. That was at least the partial truth.

"I hope Cornelia and I can reconcile. I cannot bear to think that I have lost a friend."

His expression softened. "She is lucky to have a friend as loyal as you."

"We have known each other for many years. We…have been through a lot together."

"You also most admirably tolerate her selfishness and impertinence."

His gaze captured and held hers, as though there was more he intended to say. While she wondered just what he was about, he reached out and gently cupped her face with his hand. As he stroked his thumb across her skin, potent longing stirred inside her. She yearned to close her eyes and lean into his caress.

"You are a remarkable lady," he murmured.

His smoldering gaze fell to her mouth, and part of her soul leapt, urged her to rise up on tiptoes so she could press her lips to his, no matter who might see. The desire to kiss him was almost more than she could bear.

His jaw hardened, and he lowered his hand. "Careful, Honoria. Others are watching."

"I know." *I do not care. I long to kiss you again.*

"I will see you anon." Tristan's tone revealed none of the hunger she'd glimpsed in his expression moments ago. He nodded to her then strode past to join Radley.

"Any sign of the three travelers Sydney mentioned to you?" Tristan asked.

"Nay." Radley smiled at a toddler walking alongside his mother. "However, my men-at-arms are on the lookout. I have ordered them to report to me anyone who seems at all suspicious."

Tristan assessed the bailey. Opening the castle gates to any man, woman, or child who wished to enter created a prime opportunity for criminals to get into the fortress if they could evade the guards.

Radley seemed to have the situation under control, though. More than enough men-at-arms were on duty.

Near the stables, a massive log was being lifted down from a horse-drawn cart by several men: 'Twas the Yule log that would be lit with great ceremony in the hall's hearth later that night and would burn for a full twelve days. Servants went about their daily tasks, while the scents of baking fruit cakes and gingerbread wafted on the breeze. Tristan's stomach rumbled, for Radley had told him that in keeping with tradition, a feast of grilled and baked fish, periwinkles, and other seafood had been planned for that eve which was considered a fast-day; roasted meats and dishes laden with sumptuous cheese and cream sauces would be served on Christmas Day. After so much fine food, Tristan would need to add extra training sessions to his schedule once he reached London.

"Have you seen Cornelia today?" Radley asked, as he waved to a girl riding on her father's shoulders.

"She and I met in the upstairs corridor. She rushed past with a terse 'good morn.'"

"Mother has asked me what happened between Cornelia and Honoria, but I have not shared the details."

"Thank you. I would hate to be thrown out on my arse on Christmas Eve."

Radley squinted up at the dense clouds. "'Tis only

morning. You could still run afoul this day."

Shaking his head, Tristan laughed. He had no intention of running afoul. He could only hope that matters went exactly as he'd planned.

"Make way. Make way for the Yule Log!" Radley bellowed later that day as he entered the crowded hall.

Sitting at the lord's table with her mother and Guillaume, Honoria smiled and clapped, while cheers erupted in the vast room.

Burly men-at-arms, carrying the giant Yule Log between them, emerged from the forebuilding. Maidservants pulled their excited children out of the way. Dogs scampered to watch from under the two trestle tables, laden with centerpieces and sweets, that had been left standing after the evening meal had been cleared away.

Puffing and grunting, the men hauled the log across the hall and set it in the hearth. Using a small piece of last year's Yule Log, Radley set light to the wood. Flames licked up the side of the log, and more cheers filled the chamber.

"And now, may the merriment continue," Radley yelled.

The musicians at the opposite end of the hall strummed a lively song and folk moved into the center of the room to dance. Those watching made a loose circle around the revelers and clapped along with the tune, accentuated by the drumming of a tabor.

"I do love Christmas Eve," Honoria's mother said with a contented sigh. She leaned her head against Guillaume's shoulder, while his arm curved around her, drawing her in close. He kissed her brow.

Envy poked at Honoria, and she quickly looked back out across the hall. Cornelia, resplendent in a new, yellow silk bliaut given to her by her sire, was standing near the musicians and flirting with one of the squires. He appeared delighted to have her attention.

Tristan, drink in hand, was talking to Radley while they watched the dancers; some of the maidservants were revealing far more lower leg than was proper, but they *were* dancing and spinning rather vigorously.

Tristan glanced at Honoria. Smiling in that roguish way of his, he crooked a finger, motioning for her to come and join them. Wicked heat shot through her while she slowly rose and made her way down from the dais, careful not to step on the hem of her embroidered burgundy gown.

When she neared him, she caught sight of Cornelia through a gap in the crowd. The younger lady was watching, her expression fraught with dismay. Honoria lifted her hand in greeting, but Cornelia turned her back to her.

"Try not to let her bother you," Tristan said, his mouth close to her ear so she'd hear him over the revelry.

"I will do my best." 'Twas hard, though, when she had good memories of past Christmas Eves spent with the younger woman.

Across the room, a stable hand held the kissing bough, which had been taken down from the archway, over the head of a pretty chambermaid. He plucked off a white berry, and she smiled shyly as he kissed her.

Radley chuckled. "Ah, the joys of the holiday season."

"There are a lot less berries on the kissing bough than there were this morning," Honoria noted. She hoped they didn't run out; no one wanted such a disappointment on Christmas Eve.

Cornelia was headed toward the still-kissing couple. Was she going to use the bough to win a kiss from the squire?

A sudden, loud banging noise erupted from the lord's table. Guillaume stood at the edge of the dais; he hammered his goblet on the table again in a call for silence.

"Thank you," he said once the room had quieted. "I am honored to be spending this Christmas at Ellingstow with two of the women I love the most: my beautiful daughter"—he gestured to Cornelia—"and my beloved Valerie."

Clapping echoed in the hall.

"There is only one thing that could make this day more perfect: if Valerie were not just my beloved, but my betrothed."

Lady Whitford pressed her hand to her mouth. "Guillaume."

Honoria blinked hard to thwart tears, for she'd anticipated such a proposal. While 'twas difficult to think of her mother remarrying, she did want her parent to be happy.

The older lord drew a glinting ring from the leather pouch at his waist. "Valerie, my love. Will you marry me?"

She stood and walked around the table to meet him. "I will."

Guillaume smiled and slipped the ring onto her finger, and they kissed. Congratulatory shouts and whistles carried through hall.

Once the noise had died down, Tristan brushed past Honoria. He strode for the dais.

"What is he doing?" she asked, unable to tamp down a stirring of dread.

Radley grinned. "Wait and see."

Tristan stepped up onto the dais beside Guillaume

and Lady Whitford. He met the older lord's questioning stare. As though reading his thoughts, Guillaume nodded and escorted her ladyship back to her seat at the table.

"I, too, am grateful to be spending the holidays as a guest of Lord Radley Whitford, a remarkable man who has been my closest friend for many years." Anticipation swirled up inside Tristan as he looked at Honoria. "One lady in particular has made this visit extremely memorable."

Murmurs carried through the throng.

Honoria appeared both astonished and dismayed. She shook her head slightly, no doubt to discourage him from drawing her into further scrutiny. Yet, for what he intended, he wanted all eyes upon her.

"Will you please join me, Honoria?"

She was clearly reluctant, but she crossed to the dais and stepped up beside him.

"Thanks to this lovely lady's efforts, I am feeling much better after being attacked by the boar," Tristan said, facing her. She nodded in acknowledgement, clearly readying to bolt. He caught her clammy hands in his, keeping her beside him.

"Tristan," she said under her breath.

"Trust me," he answered, while Radley drew near. Giggles and murmurs spread through the onlookers, for he carried the kissing bough.

Honoria's eyes widened. "If you kiss me in front of everyone in the hall—"

"I know." Naught felt more right than to kiss her on the lips, right here, right now, and claim her for his own.

"Are you absolutely sure? I mean—"

"I am sure."

He glanced at Radley. The other lord wasn't smiling, though; he seemed grim.

Before Tristan could say a word, Radley gestured to the kissing bough.

All of the mistletoe berries were gone.
Every last one.

Floating on excitement and disbelief, Honoria suddenly sensed something was wrong. Tristan's features had hardened, and Radley…. He looked more disappointed than she'd ever seen him.

The hall had gone quiet. Too quiet.

"Cornelia," Radley muttered.

"Aye," Tristan agreed.

"What do you…?" An eerie buzzing noise filled Honoria's mind. There wasn't a single mistletoe berry left on the kissing bough.

Everyone in the hall would know what that meant: No more kisses could be stolen. She would have no choice but to refuse Tristan's kiss, and according to lore, that doomed her not to marry in the coming year.

How mortifying.

Honoria pressed her lips together, while trying to ignore the countless gazes upon her. The hurt surging inside her, however, refused to be quelled. She'd been missing her late father this eve, and then had found out her mother was going to remarry. Now she was the brunt of a mean trick in front of a room full of folk?

Several maidservants stepped forward, offering her mistletoe berries, but Honoria politely declined; those berries had already bestowed their Christmas magic on other couples. "Cornelia," she said, her voice shaking. "'Tis your doing, aye?"

Her chin at a defiant tilt, the younger woman strolled forward. "What a shame. Were you hoping to kiss Tristan tonight?"

Honoria sucked in a breath, for Cornelia's brittle tone cut deep.

Guillaume's chair scraped on the dais. "Daughter, please explain what is going on."

Anguish flickered over the younger woman's features, but her chin nudged higher.

Suddenly the situation became too much. Her vision blurring with tears, Honoria ran for the stairs.

His hands balled into fists, Tristan strode to Cornelia. The castle folk were talking among themselves, obviously shocked by what had just taken place.

He grabbed the younger woman's elbow. Ignoring her protests, he pulled her across the hall and into the antechamber.

Still holding her arm, he turned on her. "That was very mean-spirited of you."

Cornelia glared. "She was mean to me."

"Honoria has hardly been mean."

"She kissed you! She knew that I—"

"She has stood by you day after day despite your selfishness and ill temper. Do you not see how loyal a friend she's been to you? Do you really think such an exceptional friendship can ever be replaced?"

Doubt flickered across Cornelia's face. "She betrayed me."

"She fell under the same spell that I did. We never intended to have romantic feelings for one another. Yet, we do. Those feelings are genuine and undeniable."

"*I* wanted you—"

"Let me be clear," he cut in. "I have no interest in courting you. Absolutely none. *Especially* not after what you just did."

Cornelia moaned. "But—"

"If you care *at all* about Honoria, you will accept our relationship. You will be happy for her. You will apologize to her. And, by God, you will start acting like the noble lady you were born to be, not a spoiled child."

Tristan released Cornelia's arm, dislodging a handkerchief that had been tucked into her sleeve. The embroidered square of silk fell to the rushes. She stared at him, tears filling her eyes, before she stormed out into the hall.

He picked up the handkerchief, set it on the table, and then plowed his hand into his hair. He might as well go and pack his saddlebag, after what he'd said to her. She was no doubt running to her father for consolation, and Guillaume wouldn't tolerate his beloved daughter being upset.

The music and dancing had resumed in the hall, but Tristan didn't feel like returning to the celebrations. He wanted to kiss Honoria. He was going to have that special moment with her under the kissing bough, despite Cornelia's interference, before he was thrown out in disgrace. He knew where to get plenty more mistletoe.

He strode out of the antechamber, wove through the revelers, and loped down the forebuilding stairs. When he pushed open the door to the bailey, icy air and fat snowflakes swirled in from the darkness. The snow was falling heavily; he could barely see across to the kitchens and stables. He'd be a fool to try and reach the garden in such conditions.

As he made his way back up to the hall, Willow appeared at the top of the stairs. The wolfhound studied him, brown eyes catching the torchlight. When he brushed past, the dog fell in beside him. Willow must be lonely with

Honoria gone from the hall.

Seeing Cornelia talking with Radley and her father, her face blotchy from crying, Tristan returned to the antechamber for her handkerchief. He might be furious with her, but he didn't want her to lose her expensive hanky, and she looked like she could use it.

Willow, still at his side, sniffed the floor near one of the front table legs. A bit of food must have fallen off a platter at some point and the dog had found it.

Willow pawed at the rushes and gazed up at him.

Really gazed at him, as if to say, 'Can you not see it?'

Amongst the churned up rushes was an object slightly smaller than Tristan's thumbnail: a mistletoe berry.

Chapter Twelve

Honoria shoved open the door of her chamber and hurried inside. Releasing a pent-up sob, she slammed the wooden panel behind her and strode for the trestle table and the waiting jug of spiced wine. In her wildest imaginings, she'd never thought Christmas Eve would turn out so—

Her skin prickled in warning.

She wasn't alone.

She abruptly halted. Barely a handful of paces away, a man in a hooded cloak rose from her open linen chest. He'd been rummaging through her possessions. A leather bag hung from a strap slung over his shoulder to hold whatever items he chose to steal. Indignation flared, but as he faced her, dread slid through her like a melting chunk of ice. He was the man from the market; the one with the scarred face.

Her pulse racing, she took a cautious step back. If she called for help, would anyone hear her? The noise from the hall would surely overwhelm the sound of her voice.

"Who are you?" she demanded. How had he gotten past the castle guards? If only there was an object close by that she could use as a weapon if needed, but the only things within reach were her father's books, no longer neatly stacked as she'd left them.

The stranger raised his callused hands, palms up, and started toward her. "Milady—"

"Why are you in my chamber, going through my things?"

He continued to advance. "I can explain."

Oh, he would, to Radley and his men-at-arms. Just a few more backward steps, and she'd yank the door open.

He lunged.

Shrieking, Honoria grabbed hold of the door handle, but his arm snaked around her waist, and he hauled her back against his body. His hand, smelling of the linen chest's metal lock, clamped over her mouth. She struggled, kicked, and dug her nails into his hand, but then the tip of a dagger pressed against her neck.

She froze.

"I do not want to hurt you," the man said, his words hot against the side of her face. "I will remove my hand, and you will not scream. Agreed?"

She would *not* agree. Given the slightest chance, she was definitely going to scream. The damsels in the old tales would not miss a chance to warn others of a dangerous intruder.

Who was this man, though? His manner of speaking bespoke a privileged upbringing—

His hand tightened on her face, and she drew in a sharp breath. "If you cry out, I will have no choice but to kill you. I do not want to take your life, but I will. Nod if you will heed my demands."

What choice did she have? She didn't want to die. When he lifted the knife slightly away from her skin, she nodded.

"A wise decision." His hand dropped away from her face, but his arm locked like an iron band around her waist. "Now, tell me where you have hidden the book."

He'd gone through her other tomes, so the only one he could mean was the book she'd bought in the market.

"You bought it at Wylebury days ago."

She resisted the impulse to glance at the bed. Last night, when she'd found it impossible to sleep, she'd read the tome by candle and firelight; when at last her eyelids had grown heavy, she'd tucked the book under the pillows beside her. The servants, while making the bed, had folded the blankets so there was no clue that anything was hidden—as they were used to doing, since she often stowed books under her pillows.

"Why is that book so important?"

"Never mind. Where is—?"

A knock sounded on the door. "Honoria?"

Cornelia. Oh, God!

The man's hand clamped over Honoria's mouth again. "Quiet," he whispered.

Remaining still, she fought the urge to bite his palm. If she acted rashly, Cornelia might be drawn into the situation. While Honoria was upset with the younger woman, she'd never forgive herself if Cornelia was injured or even killed.

Another knock. "I know you are in there," Cornelia called. "I need to speak with you."

The stranger muttered under his breath. He was clearly hoping that the younger woman would go away.

"All right. If you will not open the door...I will let myself in."

Nay! Cornelia, nay!

The door swung inward. When Cornelia saw Honoria trapped in the stranger's grip, she gasped.

"Scream, and I will slit this lady's throat," the stranger said. "Come in and shut the door. Now."

Her face ashen, Cornelia hurried in and closed the panel. "Who are you? What are you—?"

"I want the book from the market. Where is it?"

Cornelia's hand fluttered to her throat. "How would I know?"

The stranger growled. "If you are lying—"

"I am not." She sniffed in disdain. "I have no interest in books." While she spoke, her gaze met Honoria's; a silent promise that she would do her best to summon help.

"Come here."

Fear flickered in Cornelia's eyes. "Why?"

"Do it, or I will kill—"

Visibly trembling, the younger woman walked closer. Honoria tried to catch Cornelia's attention, to warn her to beware, but the man abruptly released her and pushed her, hard. She landed face down on the planks. As she scrambled to her feet, she saw that Cornelia was now the man's captive, the dagger against her neck.

"Honoria," the younger woman whispered in terror.

"Release her," Honoria said, "and I will give you the tome. I promise."

The stranger shook his head. "The book. I will not ask again."

The man's visage was so fearsome, so devoid of any trace of compassion, Honoria went straight to the bed and withdrew the tome from beneath the pillows. Crossing her arms over the book, she waited, granting him the illusion of control.

A hard smile curved the man's lips. "Bring it to me."

Honoria skirted the end of the bed, but then halted. "You will let Cornelia go."

"I give the orders. Bring it—"

Honoria shifted her arms, as though to adjust her hold on the book. It tumbled from her grasp and fell on the floor by her feet. "Oh, how clumsy of me."

The man shoved Cornelia aside and lunged for the tome.

Honoria kicked it under the trestle table. The book slid on the planks and with a *thump*, hit the wall.

"Run, Cornelia!"

"But, you—"

"*Run!*"

Cornelia bolted for the doorway, yanked it open, and raced out. "Help!" she screamed. "Someone, help!"

"That will cost you, milady," the man snarled as he came out from under the table, still holding the knife. Shoving the book into his bag, he started toward her.

Honoria dashed for the doorway, but he pursued and caught her right arm. She screeched, writhed, but his fingers didn't relax their merciless grip. She clawed at the embrasure, trying to find a handhold, but he yanked her backward. With a pained breath, she slammed against him. The dagger again pressed against her skin.

"You will never leave this keep," she said between clenched teeth.

His left arm around her, he forced her out into the passageway. "I will. You will ensure that I do."

The handkerchief in his open palm like a peace offering, Tristan approached Radley and Guillaume, who had moved to the table of sweets. Cornelia was gone. A sinking feeling settled within Tristan as he neared the men, for he could only pray this conversation didn't end with him out in the snow.

Radley was eating a mince pie. "Tris," he said around a mouthful. "I was wondering where you had gone."

Tristan held out the handkerchief to Guillaume, who frowned as he took it. "'Tis Cornelia's," Tristan said. "I realize, milord, that my private words to her were harsh—"

"They were," Guillaume agreed.

"—and that I upset her greatly—"

"You did."

He'd end up frozen in the snow tonight for certain, but Tristan would not retreat from what must be said. "She needed to understand—"

"—the foolishness of her behavior. I know."

"Aye," Tristan said slowly, "and—"

"Someone—*I*—should have said what you did much sooner."

Astonishment whipped through Tristan. "Milord?"

Guillaume shook his head. "'Tis all my fault. After the accident, I…coddled her. I was afraid to be too strict with her, while she was obviously grieving. I wish now that I—"

Movement on the landing snared Tristan's attention. Cornelia was standing at the rail, waving her arms. She was shouting; her words were drowned by the music.

"Milords." Tristan pointed.

"God's blood," Guillaume said. "What is she—?"

"She needs help." Radley ran toward the stairs.

"Help?" Guillaume asked. "Why?"

Cornelia glanced behind her, jumped as though startled, and raced for the staircase. As Tristan hurried after Radley, Honoria appeared on the landing—in the imprisoning grip of a man with a knife. When the intruder looked down into the hall, torchlight illuminated his scarred face. Tristan recognized the man from the market.

Rage boiled inside Tristan. His instincts about the man had been right all along. He reached for his sword, but he'd left all of his weapons in his chamber. He hadn't expected to need them on Christmas Eve.

He glanced at Guillaume, to ask if the older lord had a weapon, but Guillaume was elbowing his way toward the musicians, trying to catch their attention. The music faltered and then stopped.

Tristan reached the bottom of the stairs. Radley had

already scaled them and, standing at the top, had put himself between frightened Cornelia and the man forcing Honoria along in front of him. Radley hadn't drawn a weapon; he'd likely left his in his room, too.

Men-at-arms with drawn swords had gathered around the bottom of the staircase, awaiting orders.

"Out of my way," the man said as he neared Radley.

Tristan scowled at the intruder's arrogance. His tone suggested he was used to issuing orders and others immediately doing his bidding, which meant he must be a nobleman. No chivalrous lord of the realm, though, would hold a damsel hostage.

Honoria looked scared, but determined to survive her ordeal. Admiration for her coursed through Tristan, for she had stronger mettle than most ladies he knew.

"Let my sister go," Radley said, his voice cold and even.

"She comes with me. Do not try to stop me from leaving this hall, or I will kill her." The stranger shoved her back to a walk; she was now only a few paces from her brother.

"He has the book I bought," Honoria choked out. "'Tis in his bag."

His mind racing, Tristan climbed the lowest steps. "What does he want with the tome?" he called.

"I do not know," she answered shakily.

Tristan vowed to get the book. The stranger wouldn't have gone to such extreme measures on a snowy Christmas Eve, of all nights, unless there was something extremely damning in its pages.

"You will never reach the forebuilding," Radley said. "Surrender."

"Move, or I will slay her *now*." The knife shifted higher, to rest near her throat. One nick, intentional or accidental, and her life was over.

Tristan would *not* let her die. If 'twas the last thing he ever did, he'd save her from this peril. He had a better chance of vanquishing her captor, though, once the man had descended to the hall.

"Mayhap we should heed him," Tristan called up to Honoria's brother. As Radley's astounded gaze met Tristan's, he stole a quick, sidelong glance at the men-at-arms. He could only hope Radley understood.

"I will not let him leave with my sister." Radley's tone was the perfect blend of desperation and fury.

"What choice do we have?" Tristan forced defeat into his voice. "He has outwitted us."

Chapter Thirteen

H onoria stumbled along in the stranger's hold, the garlicky stink of the man's sweat surrounding her. Surely Tristan didn't mean what he'd just said: that they should concede to this criminal's demands? Indignation warred with her fear, for she didn't want the stranger to triumph this day, especially if he intended to keep holding her hostage and take ownership of her book.

Knights always vanquished villains, did they not? So why weren't Tristan or her brother trying to free her?

As she was forced past Radley, she met her brother's stare. He was clearly worried, but there was also a glint of cunning in his eyes. Mayhap he and Tristan had a plan, after all.

The stranger maneuvered her down the steps. Moving with care, so she didn't slip on her gown's hem and get cut by the knife, she dared a glance across the hall that was utterly silent. Folk watched, their expressions fraught with concern.

Guillaume had his arms around her mother. A frantic-looking Cornelia stood beside them; thankfully she was safe.

Booted footfalls sounded behind her and the intruder: Radley was following them down the stairs. Knowing her brother was so near sent hope blooming inside her. She must be ready to run, to fight off this man, when she had the opportunity.

At the bottom of the stairs, Tristan waited. His face was a mask of carefully controlled anger. He looked frightening, powerful, and so very handsome.

Her father would have liked Tristan. Her eyes burned, for there was much she wanted to say to Tristan, to share with him, and she *was* going to say and do those things. The man with the scarred face wasn't going to ruin her chance at true love.

When they reached the lower steps, Tristan, his mouth a grim line, stepped aside to let them pass. The men-at-arms also stepped back. Radley must have signaled for them to do so. She hardly dared to breathe, for the sense of expectation—of simmering violence about to erupt into chaos—hung heavily in the air.

Her shoes crunched on the dried rushes and herbs scattered on the hall floor. As the man forced her onward, Willow loped over from the hearth. Hackles up, the dog snarled. Honoria had never seen the hound in such a state, but then she'd never been in grave danger before.

"Call off the dog," the stranger shouted, "or it dies."

"Go, Willow," she called.

Radley whistled. "Here, Willow."

Snarling, the dog leaped for the man's right arm.

The intruder lashed out with the dagger.

Honoria shoved him, hard.

With a strangled curse, the stranger staggered sideways, the wolfhound locked onto his arm. Kicking at the dog, the man tried to switch the dagger to his other hand.

Racing past Honoria, Tristan tackled the stranger. The two men fell to the floor, the dagger flashing as they fought for it. Honoria desperately hoped that Tristan wouldn't be stabbed; he was at a disadvantage being injured from the boar hunt, and the man with the scarred face was strong.

Willow barked fiercely, while the men grunted and wrestled, shreds of dried rushes clinging to their clothes. Honoria, now at a safe distance with her mother, Guillaume, and Cornelia, called the dog to her side. Reluctantly, the hound obeyed.

Her brother and his men-at-arms closed in. "I want the intruder alive," Radley ordered.

The man with the scarred face broke free from Tristan and lurched to his feet. The intruder had lost the knife. Honoria cried out in relief.

The stranger ran toward the forebuilding, but Radley and the guards swiftly encircled him, their swords pointed at his torso.

Glowering, the intruder halted and held up his hands in surrender.

The folk in the hall cheered and whistled.

Radley took the intruder's bag and handed it to Tristan, before the guards pinned his hands behind his back and tied them with the leather cord Tristan had handed them—the cord that had held his pouch with Odelia's lock of hair.

Tristan met and held Honoria's gaze, and she smiled. He smiled back.

How grateful she was for his bravery. She couldn't wait to thank him properly.

"Who are you?" Radley demanded, once the intruder was secured. "Why did you break into my keep and steal my sister's book?"

The man sullenly averted his gaze.

"I can answer part of that question," Guillaume said. "I believe he is John Putnam, the youngest of the four Putnam sons."

Tristan stilled, his fingers curling around the pouch of hair. He could not have heard Guillaume correctly. The intruder's last punch to the head, the one that had made Tristan's ears ring, must have affected his hearing.

"Can you say that again?" Tristan asked, while he shoved the pouch under his belt for safekeeping.

"He is John Putnam, the youngest brother of your former fiancée."

"Odelia's *brother*?" Tristan hadn't met all of her siblings; the two youngest had been in Scotland, on missions for the crown. Now that Guillaume had mentioned her name, though, Tristan did see a resemblance between Odelia and this man in the set of his eyes and shape of his mouth.

"Are you John Putnam?" Radley demanded.

The intruder remained silent.

"He will not readily admit his name," Tristan said; the uncompromising set of the man's jaw revealed a great deal. "He knows that once we confirm his identity, the reputation of his entire family will be tainted by his dishonor." How damned ironic that Tristan understood exactly how the man felt.

"I have only met John a couple of times, but I am quite sure 'tis him," Guillaume insisted.

Even as Tristan struggled to grasp all of the ramifications of the revelation, Sydney and four men-at-arms entered the hall, their cloaks dusted with snow. Between them, hands bound, trudged two men Tristan had never met before.

"Guards discovered these intruders on the rear battlement, milord," Sydney said to Radley. "They had scaled the wall using an iron hook and rope. They had also subdued the men-at-arms on duty there."

"God's blood," Radley muttered. "I want the whole castle searched for intruders. The outer grounds as well."

"The captain of the guard has already begun a search, milord."

"Good. I await his report. Any injuries?"

"The men who were subdued are unconscious, and have been taken to the garrison. Milord, guards identified these men as two of the riders I reported to you earlier." Sydney's gaze found John. "He might be the third."

"You were right to be suspicious of them. What we do not know is what these men wanted." Radley glared at the captives. "Who sent you? What were you looking for, and why?"

The men remained silent.

"With your permission," Tristan said, holding up the book, "I will see if I can find out."

"Do it."

Tristan glanced at Honoria, who was embracing her mother. His heart constricted at the thought of how close he'd come to losing her. They would find whatever was so important in her book. Together.

"Secure the captives in the dungeon," Radley said to the men-at-arms. "See if you can get any answers from them. I will join you shortly."

"Are you sure you are all right?" Lady Whitford asked, squeezing Honoria's hands.

"I am fine. I promise."

"Tristan was magnificent the way he came to your rescue." Her mother winked. "I knew he was remarkable the moment I met him."

Honoria smiled. For once, regarding men, she agreed with her mother.

When Lady Whitford moved away, Cornelia rushed in, wrapped her arms around Honoria, and hugged her tight. "I was so afraid for you," the younger woman said. "I am grateful you were not hurt."

Honoria hugged Cornelia back. "I am glad you are all right, too."

Drawing away to arm's length, the younger woman shuddered. "When I saw you in your chamber, with that knife at your throat—"

"'Tis all right. You do not need to say more."

"Oh, but I do." Cornelia's expression turned earnest. "What Tristan said to me.... His words made me see how wrong I had been, in a great many ways."

Honoria had no idea what Tristan had said to the younger woman, but he'd obviously made an impression.

"When I realized you might be hurt or killed, naught was as important to me as your life. I did not want to lose you. I simply *could not*. You have been such a generous friend, and I...I am sorry for being so horrible to you tonight."

Honoria could hardly believe what she was hearing, but she was grateful for the apology. "Thank you, Cornelia."

"I have been selfish and spiteful. Well, no more." The younger woman's lips formed a wobbly smile. "I am going to work hard to be a better person. I want to be a brave, clever, honorable lady just like you."

"You already *are* brave. You alerted everyone in the hall to the intruder."

Cornelia's eyes shone. "That was rather brave, was it not?"

"Just like a damsel from one of my books."

"Oh, Honoria." There was no censure in the younger woman's voice; only admiration. "Mayhap sometime, I can borrow that book? I have decided I would like to read the old stories."

"I would be happy to let you borrow it."

As they embraced again, armed guards hurried past, headed for the keep's upper level, no doubt undertaking the search that had been ordered.

Tristan approached, carrying the tome. His tender gaze skimmed over Honoria. "You are well? Unhurt?"

"Aye, I am well." She wanted so desperately to throw herself into his arms and kiss him. Did she dare?

"Wait just a moment you two." Cornelia dashed off into the crowd that had resumed mingling.

Tristan stepped closer. Far too close to be gallant.

He skimmed the backs of his fingers down her cheek, a touch so gentle, Honoria thought she might swoon. "Tonight, may I dance with you?"

She couldn't tear her gaze from his. "You may. Also, I—"

Cornelia rushed up beside them, her hands behind her back. A little breathlessly, she said, "Honoria, hold out your hand."

"Why? And what are you hiding behind your back?"

The younger woman giggled. "Just hold out your hand."

When she did, Cornelia dropped a small object into Honoria's palm: a mistletoe berry.

Tristan chuckled and held up another white berry between his thumb and forefinger. "Willow helped me find this one."

"Willow?" *Oh, mercy.*

With the rustle of greenery and ribbon, Cornelia drew the kissing bough out from behind her back. Radley, who must have seen what she was doing, strode over and lifted her up, sitting her on his shoulder so that she could hold the bough over Honoria and Tristan's heads.

"I guess this means we are going to kiss," Honoria murmured.

"What an excellent idea." Tristan's strong arm slid around her waist, and he pulled her flush against him. She lifted her chin and his mouth descended upon hers.

Oh, God. Oh, good heavenly gracious....

Her mind went blank as she surrendered to the incredible pleasure. His lips moved gently, skillfully, but with definite purpose, as in his chamber: He was teasing her into craving more. And she *did* want more. Her whole body sang with the joy—the *rightness*—of kissing him.... He made her feel cherished. Complete. As if they belonged together, now and forever, like the knights and damsels of lore.

She became aware of cheering and whistling. When the kiss ended, and she opened her eyes, she saw they were surrounded by castle folk, including her mother and Guillaume.

Tristan pressed his forehead to hers and grinned down at her. "That was some kiss, milady."

"'Twas the perfect kiss under the kissing bough, milord."

"One more, and we will go inspect your book. Radley wants to find out why 'tis so important."

"We could do that now."

Tristan growled. "Kiss me again, or I swear, I will—"

Laughing, she rose on tiptoes and crushed her mouth to his.

Moments later, Honoria surfaced to hear a renewed burst of revelry. When she drew back from Tristan, though, she realized Cornelia no longer held the kissing bough above them.

Glancing over her shoulder, Honoria found the younger woman in her brother's arms. They were kissing!

"You were incredibly brave," Radley said, gazing into Cornelia's eyes.

"So were you," she whispered.

Smiling, Honoria leaned in against Tristan's broad chest. Cornelia might have found a lord to love her, after all.

Chapter Fourteen

Tristan studied the tome lying open on the lord's table. Guillaume, Lady Whitford, and Cornelia stood close by, while he and Honoria examined the book from cover to cover. Before Radley returned from the dungeon, Tristan hoped to have the answers they all wanted.

The top right corners of the tome were battered, likely damaged when it had hit the wall in Honoria's chamber, but the rest of it was as he remembered.

Tristan turned more pages. He did not see aught suspicious; not unless the lady's writings contained some kind of secret code. That would require taking the book to London, to be passed on to an expert who—

"Wait." Honoria leaned in closer, her finger trailing along the back cover. "This section that was repaired."

Tristan turned to the back cover. Several of the stitches had torn.

His mind buzzed. "Mayhap John was not worried about what was written in the book, but what might fall *out* of it."

Honoria's eyes widened.

He pulled out more of the stitches and drew the pieces of leather apart. Honoria gasped, reached in, and took out a folded sheet of parchment, which she flattened out on the table between them.

"What is it?" Guillaume asked, moving in with Lady Whitford to better see.

"Aye, do tell us," Cornelia said excitedly.

The parchment bore a list of dates, some less than a sennight away; names of crown officials and lords, including John Putnam's; descriptions of specific bends and parts of forest roads—

"God's blood." Tristan's innards grew cold.

"What does it all mean?" Honoria asked.

"If I am reading this correctly, these are instructions for ambushes."

"*Ambushes*?" Guillaume echoed.

Tristan nodded grimly. "This man"—he pointed to a name on the parchment—"is responsible for gathering taxes in this part of England. He is good at his job, and as you can imagine, he is despised by many. With him dead—"

"The King would appoint another to take his place," Honoria said.

"Aye, but 'twould take days or even sennights. Moreover, if the attackers stole the collected tax money that would have ended up in the crown's coffers, they could use it to pay men to rise up against the King in armed revolt."

"Mother Mary," Lady Whitford whispered. "My dear Lewis always feared there would be such an uprising."

"Why are these lords plotting attacks?" Guillaume asked with a frown. "Why do they not write up their grievances and request an audience with the sovereign or his ministers?"

"From all I have heard, some have tried, and have had little success. By slaying crown officials and lords who are loyal to King John, the discontent nobles hope to sway the balance of power in England."

Her thoughts racing, Honoria found John Putnam's name again on the page. "This man who wanted my book—"

"Is in charge of the attack planned for the seventh

day of January."

"I am guessing he intended to buy the tome to get his instructions, except I purchased it first?"

"Exactly. He couldn't get the book from you in the market without attracting unwanted attention or being arrested, so he waited until he could get inside the keep and steal it." Tristan scowled. "I expect he was the main contact in this area. He would pass on details of the ambushes to other lords, including the two who accompanied him this eve, who would also carry out attacks."

"What about the peddler?" Honoria asked. "Was he involved too?"

"Mayhap, but I doubt it. I suspect he had no knowledge of the missive or the ambushes. Someone likely gave him the book and paid him to sell it in the market, where John was to buy it. The peddler agreed because he needed the money."

"We must get this document to London," Guillaume said, "as swiftly as possible. There must be other lords involved in this treachery whose names are not on the parchment. They must be identified and captured, before 'tis too late."

Tristan nodded. "Radley will reach the same conclusion."

A sickening realization made Honoria press her hand to her stomach. She hardly dared to speak the words, for they would upset her mother, but she must. "Father died after an ambush. He was accompanying a crown minister. Do you think…?"

Tristan's gaze held hers. "If you are asking whether the men on this list might be responsible for your sire's death—"

"Aye."

"I expect so. If they are not, they will know the men who are."

Chapter Fifteen

Late afternoon, six days later

Cornelia raced into the great hall. "They are back! Radley and Tristan are back."

Sitting by the still-decorated hearth with Willow and her mother, who was dozing with her embroidery in her lap, Honoria set down her book. Happiness swirled up inside her, for she'd missed Tristan so much.

They'd all attended the traditional Shepherd's Mass at dawn on Christmas Day. However, before the gift-giving, the magnificent feast, the Mass of the Divine Word, and the rest of the merrymaking, Radley had sent missives to the local sheriff as well as the lords and crown officials who, according to the parchment, were going to be ambushed. The following day, with the snow beginning to melt, Radley, Tristan, and eight heavily-armed guards had taken the document and the three captured men to London, to be handed over to the King; no other intruders had been found in the search on Christmas Eve. With luck, all of the attacks that had been planned had been thwarted.

Disquiet gnawed at Honoria as she set aside her tome and stood. What if in their days apart Tristan had decided he didn't love her as much as he'd thought? He'd told her before that he was going to start a new position in London. He might want to remain unattached so he could start afresh in the great city.

If that was so, then their love wasn't destined to be after all. She would let him go. Regardless of any commitment that had been forged by their kiss under the kissing bough, she cared for him too much to force him to wed her.

Honoria went with Cornelia to the bailey. The younger woman had changed so much since Christmas Eve; she was a much happier person altogether.

"Cornelia." Radley handed his destrier's reins to a groom, threw his arms around her, picked her up, and twirled her around. She squealed in delight before kissing him.

"Good afternoon, my love," Tristan murmured.

My love. How Honoria loved that endearment. He leaned down and kissed her, a long, slow, most tantalizing kiss that made her want to be his forever.

"Your journey went well?" she asked, trying not to think of the important conversation they must have later.

"Better than we had hoped." Tristan slung his saddlebag over his shoulder. "The King granted us both special commendations for bringing the men and the parchment to him."

"How wonderful!"

Smiling, Tristan kissed her again. "I am hoping my sire will be impressed when he hears of it."

"I am sure he will be." She linked her arm through Tristan's. "Also, when your father finds out Odelia's brother is a traitor, he will be glad you did not marry her. You saved your family from being drawn into a scandal."

"True. Hopefully now, my sire and I can resolve our differences. By the way, the King told me you should expect a letter from him soon."

Her pulse jolted. *She* was to receive a letter from the sovereign? "Really? Why?"

"You saved many lives by purchasing that tome. You

might even have prevented a war."

She'd never have believed that what was hidden in a book could affect all of England—not until this Christmas.

They walked to the keep, Cornelia and Radley a short distance behind them.

In the hall, Lady Whitford greeted the men warmly and ordered a servant to bring mulled wine. "Guillaume sends his regards," she said. "He returned to his fortress several days ago, but will be back at Ellingstow this evening. He is anxious to know what happened in London."

"We will be glad to tell you what we can," Radley said, setting down his saddlebag.

To Honoria, Tristan said, "I have something you must see. A surprise."

"What kind of surprise?"

Radley grinned. "One you are sure to like."

As everyone gathered round, Tristan set his saddlebag on the nearest trestle table and pulled out a rectangular, cloth-wrapped object. "For you, my love."

A heady thrill rippled through Honoria as she set the parcel down. She drew back the fabric to reveal a tome with an exquisite, tooled-leather cover. "Oh, Tristan!"

"This one's extra special," Radley said, his arm around Cornelia's waist.

Honoria's hand trembled as she opened the front cover. *The Romance of Tristan and Honoria* was written in elegant script on the front page. Beneath the title were two beautifully painted figures: a knight in chain mail armor and a lady in a flowing gown, facing each other and holding hands. Tristan must have commissioned the book while he was in London.

Cornelia cooed. "How incredibly romantic."

"And perfect," Honoria's mother murmured.

'Twas indeed a perfect and most thoughtful gift. When Honoria turned to the next page, and the next, though, she saw they were blank. "Why——?"

"The story of our love is yet to be written," Tristan said.

Her stomach somersaulted as she met his gaze. "Are you certain about us? We have only known each a short while——"

"And yet, in our hearts and souls, we have known each other forever."

They had indeed. Oh, he was going to make her weep, saying such lovely things.

Tristan caught her hand and kissed it, before dropping down on one knee before her. He reached into the leather bag at his hip and withdrew a gold band inlaid with gemstones.

Honoria gasped.

"Lady Honoria Whitford, will you be my beloved damsel for the rest of our lives? Will you do me the honor of becoming my wife?"

I will. Oh, I will. How she wanted to immediately agree, yet she had to be absolutely sure about the decision. "Can I keep Willow and my books?"

He laughed. "Of course you can. That dog is your devoted protector. As for the books, we will start our own collection. We can read the stories to our children."

Her heart soared. "I would like that." Remembering the tomes from his youth that his sire had ruined, she said, "Mayhap in London we can find a craftsman to repair your books, so they can become part of our collection."

"Agreed." Still down on one knee, he asked, "So, my love, is that an 'aye'?"

Tears in her eyes, she nodded. "Most definitely an 'aye.'"

He slid the ring onto her finger. When he stood, she threw her arms around his neck and soundly kissed him.

Cornelia squealed.

Honoria's mother sniffled and wiped her eyes. "Oh, Honoria, your father would be so thrilled for you."

"Many congratulations, you two." Radley said. "Now, if I may, I have something to ask Cornelia." He dropped down on one knee on the rushes in front of the younger woman and presented her with a gold ring set with a blue gem the color of her eyes.

"Radley?" the younger woman whispered.

"Will you be my wife?" he asked solemnly. "I have loved you since we were children, although it took the danger on Christmas Eve for me to realize just how much. We can have a fine life together, if you are willing."

"I am."

Radley put the ring on her finger and stood. They kissed.

"Three betrothals in just a few days," Honoria's mother said. "Who would have guessed?"

With a contented sigh, Honoria gazed up at her husband-to be. "This has been a remarkable holiday."

"It has indeed." He kissed her, so tenderly. "You might like to know that when we were riding to London, I threw the pouch with Odelia's hair into a river. There was no sense holding onto it any longer. The vow I had made to myself was pointless, because my destiny is to be with you."

"Oh, Tristan, I love you." Those words didn't come close to conveying how much she treasured him or how truly happy she was.

"I love you, too." He winked. "In the coming weeks and months, we will fill our book with incredible stories. We might start with our first meeting in the market and how the mischief of this year's kissing bough ended up with us getting betrothed."

Honoria smiled. "What a good idea. 'Tis quite an extraordinary tale, indeed."

About Catherine Kean

Award-winning author Catherine Kean's love of history began with visits to England during summer vacations, when she was in her early teens. Her British father took her to crumbling medieval castles, dusty museums filled with fascinating artifacts, and historic churches, and her love of the awe-inspiring past stuck with her as she completed a B.A. (Double Major, First Class) in English and History. She went on to complete a year-long Post Graduate course with Sotheby's auctioneers in London, England, and worked for several years in Canada as an antiques and fine art appraiser.

After she moved to Florida, she started writing novels, her lifelong dream. She wrote her first medieval romance, *A Knight's Vengeance*, while her baby daughter was napping. Catherine's books were originally published in paperback and several were released in Czech, German, and Thai foreign editions. She has won numerous awards for her stories, including the Gayle Wilson Award of Excellence. Her novels also finaled in the Next Generation Indie Book Awards, the National Readers' Choice Awards, *InD'tale* Magazine's RONE awards, and the International Digital Awards (twice).

When not working on her next book, Catherine enjoys cooking, baking, browsing antique shops, shopping with her daughter, and gardening. She lives in Florida with two spoiled rescue cats.

www.catherinekean.com

Connect With Catherine

Catherine loves to keep in touch with her readers!

Newsletter sign-up
https://landing.mailerlite.com/webforms/
landing/g8a7w8

Website
www.catherinekean.com

Facebook
https://www.facebook.com/Catherine-Kean-Historical-
Romance-Author-196336684235320/

BookBub
https://www.bookbub.com/profile/catherine-kean

Goodreads
https://www.goodreads.com/author/show/
695820.Catherine_Kean

Amazon Author Page
https://www.amazon.com/Catherine-
Kean/e/B001JOZEMU/

A Knight's Desire

Lost Riches Series Book 1 By Catherine Kean

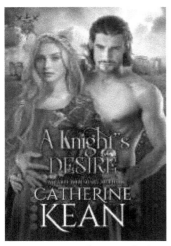

Lady Rosetta Montgomery is on her way to her wedding when she's kidnapped by a rider dressed all in black. She discovers her abductor is Lord Ashton Blakeley, her first and only true love, who left her to go on Crusade.

Ash is a changed man now, with disfiguring scars and agonizing secrets. As rumors of lost Anglo-Saxon gold and treachery unfold, and Rosetta grows to understand the man Ash has become, will she help him fight for their love, or will the danger surrounding the hidden riches cost them all that they treasure?

ISBN-10: 1724104446
ISBN-13: 978-1724104441
eBook ASIN: B07HNJRTXQ

A Knight's Vengeance

Knight's Series Book 1 By Catherine Kean

Geoffrey de Lanceau will never believe his father was a traitor. Back from Crusade, Geoffrey has vowed to avenge his sire's killing and reclaim the de Lanceau lands. When Geoffrey rescues a headstrong damsel from a near-accident and learns she's the daughter of his enemy, Geoffrey knows just how he will exact his revenge.

Lady Elizabeth Brackendale dreamed of marrying for love, but is promised to a lecherous old baron. Then she is abducted and held for ransom by a scarred, tormented rogue. He's the hero who saved her life. He's also the knight who intends to slay her father.

Elizabeth is determined to escape and undermine Geoffrey's plans for revenge, but the threads of deception sewn years ago bind the past and the present. When her father declares war, she's torn between her loyalty to him and her feelings for Geoffrey. Only by Geoffrey and Elizabeth championing their forbidden love can the truth at last be revealed about a knight's vengeance.

ISBN-10: 1092509747
ISBN-13: 978-1092509749
eBook ASIN: B006NQQ464

CPSIA information can be obtained
at www.ICGtesting.com
Printed in the USA
LVHW041325030122
707736LV00014BA/157